Books by Joe McGinniss

*The Selling of the President 1968*
*The Dream Team*

# The
# Dream
# Team

# The Dream Team

Joe McGinniss

Random House, New York

Library of Congress Cataloging in Publication Data

McGinniss, Joe.
The dream team.

I. Title.
PZ4.M14385Dr    [PS3563.A2985]    813'.5'4    73-38589

ISBN: 0-394-47992-0

Manufactured in the United States of America
by American Book–Stratford Press, New York, N.Y.
9 8 7 6 5 4 3 2
First Edition

"We . . . took off rather suddenly. We had a report somewhere around four o'clock in the afternoon before that the weather would be fine, so we thought we would try it."

—Charles Lindbergh

The
Dream
Team

# Prologue

IN LATE JANUARY of 1963, Peewee and I decided to go south. The decision was made at eleven o'clock on a Friday morning in Rinaldo's bar, at the bottom of the hill. That morning, for the first time since Thanksgiving, the temperature had risen above freezing. Trucks splashed by outside, spraying brown slush against sidewalks, buildings, and each other. We could hear the sound of their chains on wet pavement above the noise of Rinaldo's television set. A pale sun hung inertly in the sky.

I was drinking my first Rheingold of the day. For some

reason, Rinaldo charged only twenty-five cents a bottle for his Rheingold. The most prevalent theory was that he stole it off the truck. Peewee drank muscatel from a bottle wrapped in a brown paper bag. He was doing the Jumble Words in the New York *Daily News*. He looked rumpled from not having slept on sheets since September. His mother had given him four new Irish linen sheets in the fall, but they had remained in the bottom of his trunk. I think he felt that people who drank muscatel were not supposed to sleep on sheets.

Until very recently Peewee had been employed part-time as a bartender at Rinaldo's. Then one night he drove Rinaldo's daughter home from work. They were discovered on the pool table in the paneled basement at three A.M. By Rinaldo. The next day Peewee was dismissed. He never was quite sure whether his violation of the daughter, or the pool table, was the cause.

Our plan was a grand tour of thoroughbred horse-racing tracks in the south. We would drive straight to Hialeah, outside Miami. Then, after three or four days, swing around the Gulf to the Fair Grounds in Louisiana; come back through Oaklawn Park in Arkansas, on up to Charles Town in West Virginia, then Bowie in Maryland, and home.

I had never been to a race track in the south. I was excited. I had been to tracks around New York since I was twelve years old. My first was the old Jamaica. It since has been torn down and the site now contains apartment houses. You were supposed to be twenty-one to bet, but I was tall for my age.

I went alone that first day; I spent a lot of time alone as a child. I took a train, then a subway, then a crowded bus. When I finally got inside the race track, I felt as if—after a long search I had not realized I'd been making—I had found a home.

I lost $12 at Jamaica that day, including a ten-dollar bet on the favorite in the eighth. So I cannot say I got hooked because I won. Still, by the time I was fifteen I was hitchhiking to Yonkers Raceway—even though it was only a trotting track—sneaking in over the fence, and begging dimes and quarters until I got two dollars together for a bet. Invariably, I would lose and have to start over again for the next race. Once I saw Jackie Robinson in the clubhouse and asked him for a quarter. He said no.

By the time I was seventeen I had my own car and would cut classes in high school to drive thirty-five miles to Aqueduct for the afternoon. The thing to remember was always to save a quarter for the toll coming home. In college, cars were prohibited, but I hitchhiked to Lincoln Downs in Rhode Island, forty miles away. It was an ugly track, squatty and made of yellow brick. During February and March of 1962, I lost sixty-seven races in a row at Lincoln Downs. I hitchhiked back every night, cold and hungry in the dark. The countryside covered with sullen snow.

It is not surprising that the idea of watching horses race in the south had some appeal.

We left the next day, after a morning exam. Peewee drove. He had a white Rambler with a front seat that went back all the way. We stopped at his house in Nutley, New Jersey, to get money. His mother gave him $75 and the name of a good friend in Fort Lauderdale. Peewee's mother would give him anything. His father would not give him the time of day. His father was a neurologist and he had wanted Peewee to be a doctor, too. Peewee had graduated from a Jesuit military high school in New York City with a medal for having attained the highest Greek mark in his class. Peewee did not want to be a doctor. He wanted to be a landscape gardener instead.

We left Nutley with a little beer for the ride. We drove all night, taking turns sleeping on the reclining seat. We listened exclusively to country music on the radio. Our favorite song was a new one by Lefty Frizzell, called "Saginaw, Michigan."

> I was born in Saginaw, Michigan.
> I grew up in a house on Saginaw Bay.
> My dad was a poor, hard-working Saginaw fisherman.
> Too many times he came home with too little pay.

We drove through Carolina drizzle in the morning, and I was surprised to see in the afternoon that Georgia really did have red clay. We stopped for gas in Savannah after having come through the black section of the city by mistake. Peewee remarked to the attendant that the black people didn't have very good houses. The attendant said, "They don't deserve houses a-tall." We stopped for a hamburger in Daytona, feeling good about being in Florida, not realizing how far we had to go. And spent precious dollars on Florida Turnpike tolls because we wanted so badly to get there.

We rolled our windows down and both of us stayed awake. We smelled orange trees in the night and laughed for miles. At two A.M. we got off the turnpike at the southern end and found a Howard Johnson's Motor Lodge with the sign still lit. Rooms were $36 a night. We drove another hour along Route One and found a $12 room set about six feet off the road in a motel that was owned by an old man who had arthritis. Trucks passed so close to us our bed shook, but we slept.

In the morning the old man told us where the race track was. He said he would have shaken hands with us except for his arthritis. He waved goodbye, stooped and frail, his hands like Brussels sprouts. The sun was shining brightly and the air was very hot. We ate breakfast in a drugstore and I bought a *Morning Telegraph* to handicap the races. The orange juice in the drugstore came out of a cardboard carton. The woman said all the fresh orange juice was shipped north.

Hialeah was the most beautiful race track I had ever seen. The driveway was lined with giant palm trees, and inside there were flowers everywhere and hundreds of pink flamingos in a lake. We had $45 to bet. We bet $5 on a horse called Garwol at 6–5 and he won. Then we decided to bet big, to make enough to go to Louisiana.

By the sixth race we were broke. We walked out of the track to our car. It was very hot in the parking lot. No one else was leaving yet. No one else was broke. We used our last $1.25 for gas and drove to downtown Miami. It was even hotter there and there were many Cubans on the streets.

I went into the office of Manpower, Inc., the temporary help service. My roommate's father was a vice-president of the company. He had told me if I was ever broke in a strange town to go to their office and mention his name and they would put me on a job right away. I mentioned his name. They said if we would be at Pier 32 at six o'clock in the morning, we could unload banana boats all day. I thanked them and took the slip of paper that told how to get to the pier. They said it would be a good idea to buy a pair of work gloves before we started.

We walked for a long time through Miami, which looked like any other city, and sat in a park at the edge of a bay. We thought for an hour or so about what it would be like to unload banana boats all day. Then we walked back to the car and drove to Fort Lauderdale with the last of our gas and called on a friend of Peewee's mother.

She was an old woman with skin like lemon frosting. Peewee had never met her before. She asked about his family and he said they were fine. Then he gave her some advice about how to care for her garden and lawn and asked if she could loan us $20. She said the banks were closed and she didn't have $20 in her house. Peewee said maybe she could borrow it from a friend. She said people in Fort Lauderdale didn't borrow money from their friends, as a rule. Peewee said we had to have $20. When she saw we were not going to leave without it, she went to a friend's house and came back in half an hour with $20. Peewee thanked her profusely and said he would remember her to his mother. We drank up half the money in beach-front bars and spent the night in Peewee's car. The next day we lost the rest of the money at Hialeah.

The remainder of our Grand Tour of southern race tracks was divided evenly between the race track and the Western Union office in Fort Lauderdale. We wired everybody we could think of for money. Everybody except Peewee's mother. We wired my parents, and Peewee's sister in Peabody, Massachusetts, and Peewee's sister in Canton, Ohio, and Mac, the owner of Mac's Taxi Service in Scarsdale, New York, for whom I worked in the summers. The heartwarming thing was that no one refused us. STRANDED FLORIDA PLEASE SEND $25 SOONEST HELP. The man at the Western Union office said he had never seen anyone with as many generous relatives and friends. Every penny we got, except what we spent on gas and beer, we lost at Hialeah. Five more days without a winner. It was Lincoln Downs with central heat. By the middle of the fourth day we realized we were not going to Louisiana. By the end of the fifth day it looked as if we were not going home.

That Saturday night we went back to Peewee's mother's friend. As soon as she saw us she started to chain-smoke Parliament cigarettes. Peewee tried to be as nice about it as he could. Our absolute minimum was $30. Without that much, there was no point in getting into our car. Peewee smiled as he told her this. Then he took out his checkbook and said he would write her a check. Once, several years before, Peewee had had a checking account. Just in case of emergencies, he had decided to save the checks. They were wrinkled and had foodstains on them and were as worthless as our losing tickets from the track. Peewee blushed as he handed the check to the woman. She said she wished his mother would come down for a visit. He said he would do his best to persuade her. Then he told her not to cut her grass too short or it would burn, and we were off, driving straight through to Massachusetts, stealing bologna and American cheese all the way.

But Florida was not so bad. At least we were not cold. Two weeks later Peewee and I went to the annual winter carnival in Quebec. The "Mardi Gras of the North," it was called. To save money, Peewee did not put extra antifreeze in his car. When we tried to start it Sunday morning the temperature was thirty-six degrees below.

We used the last of our money for a tow to a gas station and waited all afternoon as the engine thawed and was repaired. When it came time to pay, Peewee said we had no money. No one spoke English but they understood that. Peewee started to write them a check. There was a great swell of muttering and a shaking of heads all around. I tried to call the local priest to see if he would take our check, but he was out.

With genuine sorrow, Peewee decided he would have to give them his trumpet. The repair bill was $21. The trumpet had cost $75 when he got it from his mother for Christmas the year he won the medal in Greek. She thought he had an inclination toward music and hoped the trumpet would enable him to express himself. Also, before she had married Peewee's father, she had been engaged to a trumpet player for two years. Peewee had learned to play four songs: "Reveille," "The Bunny Hop," half of "When the Saints Go Marching In," and *"Tantum Ergo,"* a Catholic benediction hymn. He played all four of these songs in the garage in Quebec on that icy gray afternoon. At the end, he offered the trumpet as payment for the car. There were tears in his eyes as he did this. The offering was refused.

We waited another hour, with the fattest of the mechanics sitting squarely on Peewee's keys. Then a cab-driver pulled into the station for gas. He spoke enough English to understand our predicament. He said he would loan us the money. Peewee embraced him. But, the driver said, he would have to take the trumpet for security. Perfectly all right, Peewee said, he would repay the loan within a week. We paid the bill and got as far as Concord, New Hampshire, before we had to give up our spare tire to pay for gas. The attendant told us to make sure we got back before the second Wednesday of the month, because the second Wednesday of the month was when he had his auction. All the spare tires people had left all month long to pay for gas got auctioned off. We never made it back. Nor did Peewee ever get his trumpet. The money he had intended to use to repay the loan was lost in a card game. Soon after, he lost the cabdriver's address.

Peewee and I hitchhiked 1,000 miles to the Kentucky Derby that spring. We had to hitchhike because Peewee's car had a flat and he couldn't afford a new tire. We hitch-hiked for twenty-four hours with a sign that said KEN

DERBY because I had forgotten how to abbreviate Kentucky. In most states, people thought we were advertising a candidate for the legislature.

We got to Louisville at six P.M. on Derby Eve. The air was warm and flowers blossomed. The first Friday evening of May. I had just become twenty years old.

I had hitchhiked to Louisville once before, the previous October, because I had been in love with a girl who went to school there. I had promised her I would come back for the Derby. Our romance had perished over the winter but I still wanted to see the race.

We showered at the YMCA for a dollar as pale queers gathered to stare. Then we put on madras sports coats and ties and went to the Brown Hotel in the center of town. We went to the bar and told everyone how far we had come and how we had traveled and how much our first Derby meant. They understood. They bought us drinks until four A.M. and then we walked three miles to the track.

Churchill Downs. On Derby morning. Before sunrise. We talked a guard at the stable gate into letting us in, telling him how far we had come. Across the track we could see the twin spires of the grandstand, and then a faint pink glow in the sky. Steam rose from the backs of galloping horses, and we ate a happy breakfast with some grooms.

We lost every race that day until the Derby. In the Derby there were three big undefeated horses: Candy Spots, No Robbery, Never Bend. I had $3.20 left. Enough for one bet and peanut butter crackers hitchhiking home.

None of the big horses would pay above 5–2. I studied my *Morning Telegraph* a little harder and found another horse named Chateaugay.

Chateaugay was undefeated, too, but he had raced only five times and never against this kind of competition. I looked at the odds board in the clubhouse. Chateaugay was 9–1. I bet him. The horses came onto the track. The band played "My Old Kentucky Home," and I cried. Chateaugay's rider sat tall in the saddle. A Panamanian named Braulio Baeza, wearing silks that were colored fawn-brown.

Chateaugay won the race. It was the happiest moment of my life.

I collected $20.80 on my bet, and then I bet the next two races and won them both. I left the track with $90. We ate roast beef for dinner and drank champagne in the Brown Hotel bar. Later we met a couple of secretaries from Fort Wayne.

Two weeks after that Chateaugay ran in the Preakness. It was impossible for me to go because I had a final examination that day. Except the night before I got to thinking about what the horse had done: he had given me the happiest moment of my life. The least I owed him was to watch him run in the Preakness. At ten o'clock that night I walked up the stairs to the third floor of the old house where Peewee lived with his muscatel and buried sheets, and found him asleep. I woke him, and by eleven we were heading for Baltimore. Hitchhiking again because he still had no tire for his car.

We were picked up by Maurice Dawson, of New Rochelle, New York, at the entrance to the New Jersey Turnpike in the morning, and drove through pouring rain to visit his brother Roy in Philadelphia. Roy was hard to find because he lived with a different woman every week. "The last one," Maurice said, "she was so ugly, it *hurt.*" Maurice said he could not go back to New Rochelle for a while because people were trying to kill him because they thought he had cheated in a card game. If he found Roy, they could go to Virginia to visit friends.

He found Roy, finally, in the rain, with a woman screaming. We waited half an hour for the liquor stores to open so Roy could buy a quart of Imperial for the trip. We got a flat tire in Kennett Square, Pennsylvania, twenty-five miles southwest. When I tried to borrow a jack from a gas station, the attendant said he would give me a jack over the head because he had seen I was riding with some niggers. We got the flat fixed anyway and drank lots of Imperial and somewhere in southern Delaware, Roy began to weep. He cried almost into Baltimore, where Maurice dropped us off near the track. We embraced drunkenly, exchanged phone numbers, and vowed to meet again. Chateaugay ran second in the race.

Three weeks later the last of the Triple Crown races was run. The Belmont Stakes. I was driving for Mac's by that time and Peewee was in New Jersey, mowing lawns. Coming back from a run to La Guardia, I heard on the car radio that Chateaugay had won. The Belmont was the longest, the hardest, and, among horsemen, the most prestigious of the Triple Crown events. By winning, Chateaugay had proved his Derby victory was no fluke. That he was a truly great horse. I was happy for the horse, but sad. I could have been there. I could have seen him. Mac would have given me the afternoon off. I hadn't asked because I had not believed that Chateaugay could win.

I got to the Kentucky Derby again in 1965. This time I did not have to sneak in. I covered it for the newspaper by which I was employed. In the press box, I met an old columnist from Baltimore. He was hung over from his train ride to Louisville the night before. He also was at the other end of the press box from the beer. I made about six trips for him, bringing him foaming paper cups, and he said he would help me get a job with his paper. I did not pick the winner that day, but two months later I got the job.

The following year the old columnist and I were assigned to the Belmont Stakes. He was to write his column, I was to write the story of the race. This was 1966, the year Kauai King, having won the Derby and the Preakness, was trying to become the first horse since Citation, in 1948, to win all three classic events.

The old columnist drank too much at the press brunch in the morning and kept drinking through the afternoon. He passed out at his typewriter before the race and could not be revived.

Afterward (Kauai King had lost) I shook him and slapped him and shouted in his ear. Our deadline was only an hour away. Finally he struggled to an upright position, belched, rubbed his eyes, and asked how much longer until the race. When I told him it was over, he cursed and asked me to get him a beer.

He drank in silence, looking out over the race track, while everyone else in the press box worked. About twenty minutes before our deadline, he stood, walked to the first row of the press box, and found a friend who was writing a column for a paper in Pittsburgh. Without a word, he took the Pittsburgh writer's carbons back to his own typewriter, laid them alongside, and started to type.

Halfway through, with our deadline less than ten minutes away, he looked up at me, cursed, and moaned. I asked him what was wrong.

"It's a sad fucking day in my life," he said, "when I've got to copy inferior shit like this."

We rode home that night on a Trailways bus. The old columnist sat next to a beautiful young stewardess from Allegheny Airlines. Her name was Mary, she was Irish, she had rich black hair and blue eyes. If he had not been sitting next to her, I might have fallen in love with her myself. The old columnist was drinking beer from a six-pack that warmed between his legs. He put his arm around the girl and sang opera all the way to Baltimore. "I Dreamt I Dwelt in Marble Halls" was his favorite. But every time he started to sing it, he would cry. Mary took the whole thing very well, though she declined his invitation to accompany him home to go swimming.

My wife met us at the bus station and we drove the old columnist home. He lived twenty-five miles out in the suburbs. When we got to his house he insisted we come in for a drink. We walked across his front yard slowly, commenting on the starriness of the night. Several years earlier he had returned late one night from a two-week road trip with the Orioles baseball team, had paid the cabdriver at the bottom of his driveway, and started walking, slightly tipsy, across the yard. He woke up thirty-six hours later in a hospital. His wife, a retired nightclub piano player, had gotten a swimming pool installed in his absence. She had neglected to mention this to him on the phone. She also had neglected to get the pool filled.

She was sleeping when we came into the house, but he made her get up to give us drinks. She served a bottle of vodka and three jelly glasses with traces of jelly and dog hairs still clinging to the sides. Four enormous dogs roamed the living room. In the kitchen, dishes were piled to the ceiling. She had used the last of the ice herself and had forgot to refill the trays. We sipped warm jelly-flavored vodka in the dark for twenty minutes. She did not want to turn on the light until she'd had a chance to wake up because she knew she didn't look good when she was sleepy. After two glassfuls of vodka she told us about a wonderful new invention for cleaning the teeth. Then she disappeared into the bathroom, returned with a Water Pic, and as the three of us sat staring at the floor, she filled it, plugged it in, and proceeded to demonstrate just how many hidden food particles could be dislodged from the teeth by the warm jet spray.

I haven't seen the old columnist in several years. I understand he is semi-retired now, working the copy desk. Peewee, I still see every now and then. He has not been to a horse race since our Preakness. He teaches Latin in a Catholic high school in New Jersey and works evenings in a delicatessen. He is married now and has two children and says he still hopes to become a landscape gardener someday.

Chateaugay, as far as I know, is standing at stud on a farm in Kentucky.

# Saturday

"I CAN'T BELIEVE this is happening," Jennifer said.

"It's happening. Call Delta. I'll pay the check."

"You're out of your mind," Barnaby Blaine said. "Don't get me wrong. I want you to come. But you're out of your fucking-a mind."

"Hurry, Jennifer," I said. "We don't have much time."

The dinner cost $76.70. San Francisco was not a cheap town. I paid with the American Express card my publishers had given me for my tour. I added wrong when I wrote in the tip, and the headwaiter tore up the slip. On the second slip, he did the addition himself.

Jennifer came back to the table. She was grinning and unsteady on her feet. She sang: "Off we go-ooo, into the wild blue yon-derrr . . ." She did not have much of a voice.

We waited outside Jennifer's apartment for a long time with the meter running. I tried to open a bottle of pink champagne. Why pink champagne, I don't remember. I never had drunk it before and I have not drunk it since. When finally I opened it, it fizzed all over the seat.

"Hey!" said the driver, turning around.

"Shut up," said Barnaby Blaine. "For the money we're paying, you're lucky we don't piss on your seat."

The driver recognized his voice. Barnaby Blaine was well known in San Francisco.

After ten minutes more we ran up the stairs to the apartment. Six red suitcases, overflowing clothes, lay open on the floor. Jennifer stood by a closet, zipping a garment bag shut.

"This is only for a week," I said. "You're not retiring down there."

"I need my wardrobe. I need it for my morale."

Blaine knelt on the suitcases to close them. "Let's go," he said. "This airport is twenty miles from town."

The ticket agent tried telling me we didn't need to fly first class. "Quite frankly, sir, when the plane is almost empty, as it's going to be tonight, there's really no advantage. Even sleeping is more comfortable in coach. You simply pull up the armrests—" He started to demonstrate with his hands.

"First class," I said. "And switch Mr. Blaine to first class."

"Yay!" Jennifer shouted. "He believes in doing things right!"

The tickets cost $752, including Jennifer's round trip. I used the credit card to pay.

I had met Jennifer for the first time at ten o'clock that morning when she had come to interview me at my hotel. She worked for a small suburban paper of which she was ashamed. In two weeks she would start with a wire service, Federated Press. She had been assigned to their bureau in Salt Lake City. The moment she stepped into my room I knew I could have her if I wanted her.

San Francisco was the last stop on my tour. I had come in Friday night, carrying a 102-degree fever from Minneapolis. The first thing my San Francisco schedule called for was a telephone interview with a radio show in Davenport, Iowa. I propped up a couple of pillows and unwrapped a Tootsie Pop. I had discovered, along about Cincinnati, that eating Tootsie Pops made me less likely to drink in my hotel room at night. The radio man called. He told me he had the largest listening audience in Quad Cities radio history. I asked him what the Quad Cities were. Davenport, Rock Island, Moline, he told me, and I forget the fourth.

He asked me questions for fifteen minutes and then he said he was going to his live lines. "So you, the listeners, can fire away, right after this message from Horncastle Chevrolet."

But nobody called. I lay there for twenty more minutes

and nobody called. Not one person in the largest listening audience in Quad Cities radio history cared enough to pick up his phone. The radio guy did three extra Horncastle Chevrolet commercials to kill time, and not even Horncastle called to say thanks. I knew it was time to go home.

I had been on the road since October 26. I had done Carson, Cavett, Griffin, and David Frost twice. I also had done William Buckley, Mike Douglas, Irv Kupcinet, Dave Garroway, Steve Allen, Phil Donohue, Regis Philbin, Dennis Wholey, and sixty-one local television shows. Also, 117 radio shows, including two with Howard Cosell.

William Buckley had turned out to be gracious. I met him in Detroit by accident the night before I was supposed to do his show. We flew to New York together, and when we landed he had his chauffeur wait half an hour until my luggage came through so he could drive me to my hotel. He said, "You'll never get a cab at La Guardia on Sunday night." I drank a bottle and a half of Hungarian white wine before his taping and he did not scare me a bit. Steve Allen was very nice, too. I really liked Steve Allen.

The book sold 150,000 copies. But my brain had turned to custard on the tour. My will and initiative were gone. All I had left were my desires.

Jennifer was not beautiful. Her legs seemed short for her torso, and there was a squareness to the shape of her face. But she was striking all the same. She had long brown hair that fell well below her shoulders, and lively blue eyes that did not just look at things but actually seemed to see. Her smile was strong, like a farm woman's hands, but there was a teasing, flirting quality to her voice. She wore a blue dress that was tight enough for me to see the points of her hips when she moved. The dress was very short, and I noticed light brown hair on her thighs. She seemed healthy, enthusiastic, and that appealed to me after so many weeks spent among people who were neither. If she had not been a reporter she could have taught a phys ed and hygiene class. Or joined the Peace Corps.

"Do you play tennis?" I asked.

She seemed surprised. "Three nights a week."

"And you swim?"

"Every day. In a pool at the YWCA."

"What else?"

"I sail every weekend. And play touch football in the fall. And of course I ski."

"Touch football?"

"Saturday mornings. For the Berkeley Barbettes. We only lost two games last year, and one of those was to boys."

"How about indoor sports?"

She blushed.

"I mean like ping-pong."

"Oh, those. Yes, ping-pong. Sure. And I played basketball in high school. I played defense."

"Would you like some champagne?"

"I'd *love* some. God, you've got style." She reached into her pocketbook and withdrew a notebook and a ballpoint pen with a plastic daisy in one end. We drank two bottles of champagne. Jennifer drank as fast as I did. She told me she was excited about the interview because she was my fan. She had become my fan from watching me on the talk shows. "Especially William Buckley. I flipped when I saw you on Buckley. The way you just sat there so cool. As if he didn't even scare you."

"He didn't. I was drunk."

She thought I was kidding. "No, really," she said. "You were fantastic. Like the whole thing didn't faze you. Like you really didn't care if you were there."

"I would much rather have been back in the restaurant drinking wine."

"That's just it. That's what's so cool. This whole thing is just a very small part of your life."

"What whole thing?"

"Fame. Success. Being on the Johnny Carson show."

I shrugged. "I enjoy it."

"God," she said, holding out her glass for more champagne. "You're too much. To take things like that in your stride. I admire you tremendously for that. You don't know me well enough to know how much that means, but there aren't many people I admire."

Naturally, I took her out to lunch.

We drank a bottle of champagne before we ordered, then ate linguini and clams and drank two quarts of Chianti while Jennifer told me the story of her life. She was the daughter of a wealthy San Francisco surgeon and oldest of five children. Her mother had taught her everything she knew. Such as, "Always dress well: it costs a little more but the rewards are almost infinite."

Jennifer stood suddenly, at the table, smoothing out her dress. "For instance. Do you know how much this dress cost?"

"I have no idea."

"Guess."

"I couldn't, Jennifer. I just can't tell about those things."

"Come on, take a wild stab."

"Forty dollars."

She sat down. "A hundred and ten. But it gives me assurance that I'll always be looking my best."

She had graduated from Berkeley a year and a half before, an anthropology major. Then she had traveled for a year. New Zealand, Tahiti, Easter Island. "On Easter Island," she said, "I almost started believing in God."

"How come?"

"The ruins. They were magnificent. I took hundreds and hundreds of pictures. I felt that man could not have accomplished that on his own. But then I realized that the question of God's existence was irrelevant. Each of us has an inborn divinity. Call it what you will. Call it a soul, if you insist."

"I don't insist."

"Easter Island taught me the magnificent potential of man. It made me realize the powers I had within me, just from being alive. When I left there, I couldn't wait to get home and start to realize my potential."

"In Salt Lake City?"

"Salt Lake City will be only for a year. Until I learn the fundamentals. Maybe only six months if I learn fast. Then I'll come back here, or maybe go to L.A. And then—oh

God, I wasn't going to talk about myself, but I can't help it—do you know what Federated Press is starting?"

"No."

"The Dream Team."

"What?"

"The Dream Team. A collection of the smartest, prettiest girl reporters in the country. They're bringing them all to New York and calling them The Dream Team. Imagine! *New York*." She pronounced the words as if they formed the name of a god that she prayed to.

"And what a team! All under thirty. All sexy and tough as nails. They'll use New York as a base. And tour the country. The world. Living and breathing the major events of our time. Writing every day about the famous and infamous, the tragic and great. From The Dream Team point of view."

She was staring at me, breathing hard. A faint film of perspiration on her forehead.

"Sounds exciting."

"I've never wanted anything so badly in my life as I want a place on The Dream Team. And everything I've wanted, I've always got."

Later we talked about New Zealand.

"New Zealand was special to me," she said. "Very special." This was toward the end of the second quart of Chianti. "It was on New Zealand that I gave the gift of my virginity."

"What?"

"That I made love for the first time with a man."

"You mean you never did at Berkeley?"

"No. I never did. I went to bed with a lot of different

boys, and I had many rich sexual experiences. Sometimes I would stay awake all night, experimenting. With a number of different partners and a number of different acts. But I never felt any of them deserved the gift of my virginity."

"Is that what your mother taught you to call it? The gift of your virginity?"

"No. That's just the way I came to think of it myself."

I nodded. "And nobody at Berkeley deserved it?"

"They wouldn't have appreciated it. They would have taken it for granted. So I decided to withhold it. I wanted my first act of total love to be considered by my partner as the most precious gift he'd ever received."

"Who was the lucky guy on New Zealand?"

"A librarian. He was fifty-one years old. He'd never seen a woman undressed before in his life."

"And he appreciated it?"

"We lived together for three months. Then I realized we had given all we could to each other. Besides, he was impotent because of guilt. But when I left him, I left behind a charcoal sketch I had made of myself lying naked on his bed. I pinned it to his pillow with a note that said goodbye. I love to draw. I make charcoal sketches of *everything*. It's one of the ways I express myself best."

I had to tape the "Raisin' Cane with Barnaby Blaine" radio program at four o'clock. Jennifer came with me to the station. She said she would write her story on Sunday, instead of sailing.

"Oh, wow," she said. "Barnaby Blaine. He's *only* the meanest interviewer in the city."

"He can't scare me. I've fought William Buckley."

"At least William Buckley is cultured. Barnaby Blaine comes at you like a bouncer in a nightclub. He's the rudest person I've ever heard. And he's supposed to be just as nasty in real life. But talk about success—God, he's got the hottest show in town."

Blaine looked about fifty years old. Not a tall man, and developing a paunch, but there seemed to linger about him a residue of strength—whether physical or of another kind, I could not tell. He had gray hair cropped short behind a hairline that had receded to the top of his head. I noticed alcohol veins in his cheeks. His voice was gravelly and he did not have the mechanical pronunciations of the professional radio man.

"You're late," he said, unsmiling.

I grinned. "I'm sorry. I got so engrossed in my luncheon conversation that I lost all track of time." I squeezed Jennifer's hand as I said this. She giggled.

"And you're drunk."

"No I'm not."

"You've been drinking."

"A little wine with lunch."

"What's in that bag?"

"Guinness Stout. I thought I might sip a couple bottles while we talked."

"Think again. This is a radio station, not a saloon."

"I've done it on lots of shows."

"You're not going to do it on mine. In fact, considering the condition you're in, I shouldn't let you on the air at all. I should just go on and say the author was intoxicated and unable to appear."

"Fine with me."

"What?"

"I said it's fine with me, Mr. Blaine. I don't care if I do your show."

"Then what the hell are you here for?"

"It's on my schedule. I go where they tell me to go."

"So that's what you are. Another of those mindless publicity machines."

I nodded. "That's what I've been since October. But I'm through. Monday I go home. At this point I couldn't care less about publicity."

"Yeah? Well, you know something, kid? At this point I couldn't care less about your book."

I shrugged. "Look, I told you. I don't care. All I want to do in San Francisco is have fun. I'm sick of talking about my book. And I'm sick of people like you who think they're something special just because they're allowed to talk into a microphone for a couple of hours a day. I've been doing this shit for four months, and I'm tired. I've got a girl here that I want to go out with tonight. The earlier I can get started the better. So if you're going to give me a hard time, you can do your goddamned show by yourself."

Blaine was chuckling. "That's probably the first time you've put six sincere sentences together in weeks."

"Months," I said. "Four months."

He laughed out loud. "Go on, get out of here. Buy the girl a drink. I'll handle the show by myself. If you went on, I'd have to rip you to shreds, and now that I see you're being honest, I don't want to do it any more."

"That's big of you, Mr. Blaine. It's no wonder you're so beloved."

He laughed again. "Where are you going? When I finish the taping I'd like to buy you a drink."

He bought me half a dozen, although, for the first few, I wished he had not come. I had gone with Jennifer to the Top of the Mark so I could sit by the window and spin slowly through the gray dusk that fell upon the city. It was a foolish thing to want to do, but I was feeling foolish. Monday, as I had told Blaine, I was going home. To my wife, whom I hardly knew any more; and to two children, who frightened me because I knew how much of me they would require, and how soon.

Whole sections of my life, of my self, I realized as I drank, had got rusty through disuse. I had been too busy for them, lost interest, discarded them. Now they lay silently in an obscure corner of my consciousness, like childhood toys stored in a seldom-used attic. Old friends, old values, early commitments to marriage and self—all had been stuffed haphazardly into cartons, the lids pushed quickly shut. I was young and hurrying toward success, and that was all I had time for.

Once my wife had complained to a newspaper editor for whom I'd worked: "He's always traveling, always writing, never thinking of the family or me." The editor had told her to be patient. The twenties, he'd said, were years spent rising to a level. In my early thirties I would find the level—I believe he called it a plateau—and start to coast. Then I would have time. Time for Little League baseball and rosebushes and a summer house and boat at the shore. He laid my life before me: measured in bags of charcoal briquets. I had always liked and respected the editor; he had given me my first big break. But I loathed him for telling her that. Loathed him because he spoke of plateaus when I thought only of peaks. It was his own weakness he was describing to my wife, and he made it seem an acceptable, indeed inevitable, way of life. Within three months I had left his newspaper. Moved across town to the competition, where the atmosphere was less fraternal, where I could concentrate, with fewer distractions, on my advancement.

What I wanted was to shoot upward through all the levels that anyone ever had envisioned for me, until finally I reached an atmosphere heady and rich enough to fill me when I breathed. In rising, of course, I would escape. Would leave behind the petty, the dull, and the lifeless who filled my days. What never occurred to me was that the higher I rose, the thinner the atmosphere became, and the harder I would have to strain to survive.

Everyone always wanted to know what I was going to do next. What did I want to be in five years. I'd moved so fast, I had used up all the easy answers much too soon. I had envisioned, at the start of my career, perhaps thirty years of satisfying effort: a reputation for integrity and skill that would spread slowly, quietly, like ripples in a pond. But my ultimate goals had been achieved before I'd scarcely begun. I still had thirty years to go and I had come to the end of my map. Dozens of roads ran off the edge and I didn't know where any of them led.

I knew the hard, metallic edge of my commitment had

turned soft, like neglected butter, beneath the warmth of strangers' praise and the heat of TV lights. I knew also what I had to do: to push on, to hone myself again, to an even finer edge; to distill my talent until it was pure and fine as a sunrise in Vermont. Not to squander it across the country on breakfasts of champagne and pleasure spasms in the night.

But what was I after? Where did I really want to go? Six times a day, in interviews, I had been asked those questions. My glib and clever answers never failed to draw a smile. But what were the real answers? I didn't know, and I was not even certain I wanted to know. I suspected they would be hard answers, answers that would make great demands upon my spirit.

So I drank martinis as the lights of the city winked on.

"Do you know?" Jennifer said after a while. "This is really an exciting moment in my life."

"Just this? Sitting here?"

"Yes." She was trying very hard to make her voice throaty and rich. She leaned closer to me, across the table. The soft light turned the lines of her face to graceful curves. "Sitting here with *you*," she said. "Feeling that maybe you're starting to think of me as more than just a reporter."

Absolutely nothing I had said to her up to that point could have given her any reason to think any such thing. Nonetheless, giddy with gin, I smiled and took her hand. "I'm glad you feel that way."

She smiled, and squeezed gently. "I hope your wife realizes what a lucky woman she is."

"Oh, I don't think she feels lucky. She hasn't even seen me for the past four months. And even when she does, well . . ."

"But just knowing. Just knowing that she *is* your wife. And being able to tell people. 'Oh, yes, well, my husband, of course, is so-and-so.' What a thrill that must be. What an honor."

Then Barnaby Blaine showed up. He said he was taking a big risk: if anyone caught him buying drinks and having pleasant conversation, it could ruin his reputation as the most disagreeable man in San Francisco.

"Don't worry," Jennifer said. "It would take more than *that* to ruin *your* reputation."

I think she resented having our idyll interrupted.

"How reassuring," Blaine said.

"Every time I listen to you my skin crawls."

"You have no idea how hard I work to achieve precisely that effect."

"I have to admit, though, it is exciting to meet you. You've become very famous out here."

Blaine smiled. "You and me, baby. With my brains and your sense of values, we could go far."

They went on like that awhile longer. I think Jennifer was trying to show me how daring she could be. Finally she asked him what he did in his spare time—play with his pet rats? No, he told her; he arranged his tapings so he would have three days off in the middle of every week so he could fly to Los Angeles. "To the race track," he said. "Santa Anita, Hollywood Park."

"You're a horseplayer?"

33

He looked at me coolly. "Play," he said, "is hardly the word. I've been betting horses for thirty-five years, but I've never considered it play."

Then he told us about his life. He had got out of the army at the end of World War II and taken a job with a newspaper in New York. "Every other kid in the city wanted to become a reporter and get famous. I wanted the copy desk. No travel, regular hours, working nights. I could go to the track every day. Trouble was, this was before they raced all year round in New York. November came and the horses went south. I thought about it for a couple of weeks and went with them. Got a job with the *Herald* in Miami. The copy desk. Same deal. Less pay, but the money didn't matter. I killed them in Florida that year. They went north again in March and I couldn't get a job in New York until July. It didn't matter. I made my living at the track. I hooked up with the *Sun,* but in November the tracks closed, so I went south again. I did it seven or eight years, and then I ran out of papers. My last year I had to work Jersey City in the north and Fort Lauderdale. This was before they built the expressways. That drive from Lauderdale to Tropical Park was a bitch. The next year I went into radio. Writing news, and working as an editor in the wire room. Seven, eight more years and I ran out of radio stations, too. That's when I came west. This is a picnic out here. Same job all year round and easier tracks besides."

"What do you mean, easier tracks?" I was always alert for that kind of news.

"I mean the bettors aren't so smart. New York, you got

to hustle, because you find something in the form, chances are half the grandstand has found it, too. They kill the price. A horse should pay ten dollars pays six. That doesn't happen out here. I don't know why. These people, I think they go out there for the sunshine and fresh air. For *fun*, for Christ's sake. Sometimes I get to feeling guilty. Like I'm stealing people's wallets at a picnic."

"You win, in other words?"

"Win? My friend, I haven't gone out there thirty-five years because I like the way it *smells*. It took me ten years to learn, but I've had only one losing year since. The year I got back from Korea. I was over there eighteen months and my speed charts got hopelessly outdated."

"How did you learn?" Jennifer asked him.

"I worked. Worked with the figures four and five hours every day. They're all there, everything you need. Right in the *Morning Telegraph* or *Racing Form*. I studied them hours a day. I still do. Every day. This is one game you've got to keep on top of."

"Gosh," Jennifer said. "That does sound like work."

"Yeah, but it's satisfying. To study and think and make decisions and then to see in a couple of minutes whether you're right or wrong. There's something clean about that. Something very clean that I like. There's no bullshit."

Then I told Blaine a few race-track stories of my own. His smile grew broader with each one.

"I am delighted," he said, "to make the acquaintance of another addict. I insist on buying dinner for you both."

The dinner lasted three hours and everyone got drunk. At the end of it I got my idea.

"Barnaby," I said. "You're not by any chance going to Santa Anita on Monday?" I was supposed to go home Monday, but for a horse expert like this I would be happy to stay another day. Especially if I had Jennifer to stay with me.

Blaine grinned. "No, I'm going further than that. My vacation started tonight. At midnight I'm getting on a plane. I'm going to spend all next week at my favorite race track in the world—the track I've been away from since 1958—Hialeah."

I sat by a window on the plane. I took out the armrest so Jennifer could sleep in my lap. Smiling, she closed her eyes and laid a thin gray blanket across her legs. I felt the warmth and pressure of her head on my lap, and I liked it. Across the aisle, buried beneath two gray blankets so all that showed was the top of his head, was Barnaby Blaine. There was a stack of newspapers on the floor beneath his seat. The past month's editions of the *Morning Telegraph*, which Blaine subscribed to. They would tell us everything we needed to know about what had been happening at Hialeah.

Blaine said he had subscribed to the *Morning Telegraph* and *Racing Form* since 1948. In his apartment in San Francisco he had 13,176 newspapers, which took up two full rooms. They contained performance records of more than 100,000 thoroughbred horses. More than seventy-five percent of which were dead.

# Sunday

THE PLANE LANDED at quarter of eight. The sun was bright, the sky blue, the air already warm.

"Mmmm," Jennifer said. "The tropics."

I moved haltingly down the steps that led from the plane. Jennifer supported my arm. I was trembling and pale and I wanted to lie down. I had been sick to my stomach twice since Kansas City. My forehead and the collar of my shirt were soaked with sweat.

"Careful," Jennifer said. "Don't let go of the rail."

I stared at her weakly, unable to respond.

"Keep moving," said a hoarse voice from the top of the stairs. "These papers are heavy."

"Wow!" Jennifer said. "Feel that sun. Mmmm. I love it, I love it, I love it. And it's not even eight o'clock in the morning. I can't wait to get to the beach."

I stumbled at the bottom of the stairs.

"Woops," Jennifer said. And then she giggled.

"Move, for Christ's sake!" said the hoarse voice above me. "I can't even see where I'm going."

When we got to the baggage claim, Blaine dropped his armload of papers on the floor. "Jesus, they're heavy," he said. I buckled beneath a wave of nausea and leaned against a pillar for support. Jennifer wiped sweat from my forehead with a handkerchief. "You look terrible," she said. I nodded. "You need a hot shower, followed by a cold, bracing swim. And maybe a few calisthenics to sweat the poisons out."

Blaine tapped her on the shoulder. "Let's go, sweetheart. Pay attention. Most of this luggage coming around is probably yours."

The ride to the hotel was not so bad as long as I kept my eyes closed. Blaine had rented a convertible. A Ford, painted fire-engine-red. He put the top down and the fresh air helped my head. All the expressways seemed new, and made of white concrete. If I opened my eyes, the glare of the sun on the concrete made me dizzy. "This is fantastic!" Jennifer shouted over the noise of the tires on the road. "I've never been to Florida before. I've never been east of Grand Junction, Colorado!"

The hotel seemed just as new as the expressways, and

built of the same concrete. It was in Miami, not Miami Beach, because Miami was closer to the race track. But it was in a secluded part of the city, on the bay. There were spacious lobbies strung together like boxcars. And two swimming pools—one salt water, one fresh. I signed for a suite for seven nights. Every room in the hotel was a suite. Forty-eight dollars a night. I would pay with my credit card at the end of the week.

The living room was the size of a high school basketball court. With wall-to-wall carpeting two inches thick. There was a bar, a refrigerator, and a picture window that ran the length of the wall on the bay side. Two king-sized beds in the bedroom, another picture window on the bay, walk-in closets, carpeted bathroom, and an electric shoe-shining machine.

"I was expecting a hotel room," Jennifer said. "But this is an estate." As soon as the bellman left, she kicked off her shoes and ran barefoot through the rooms. Looking out windows, opening closet doors, turning water faucets on and off, running her hands over table tops. Her toes curled into the carpet as she moved.

She ran into the bedroom and bounced up and down on one of the beds. Then she jumped off and ran to the bedroom window. The bay was brilliant with reflected sun. White sails dotted the horizon. The sky was a clean detergent-blue. She turned suddenly and walked toward me.

"This week will do so much," she said. "So much to enrich my life."

"Well, I hope it will enrich mine, too."

She was standing very close to me, staring, with her eyes alive and wide. Her body looked young and supple beneath her dress.

"Thank you," she said. "Thank you for bringing me here." Then she put her arms around my neck and kissed me. Enthusiastically. As if I had just won the 500-mile auto race at Indianapolis.

"I love it!" she yelled. "I love it, I love it, I love it!" She whirled away. Off to greet the refrigerator and the end tables and the four-cushion couch.

I let her close the bedroom door behind her to change clothes. I felt sick, and I lay on the living-room couch while she showered. I closed my eyes and tried to sleep so I would not have to think about what I'd done. Seven hundred and fifty dollars' plane fare, plus $350 for the hotel, plus I had to call my wife, who was expecting me home for dinner tomorrow night. I curled into a fetal position on the couch. Over the noise of the shower, I could hear Jennifer singing. A medley from *South Pacific*. I could think of only one justification for all of this. The word kept repeating itself in my mind as if it were an Oriental prayer: Hialeah . . . Hialeah . . . Hialeah.

I woke up squinting at the brightness of the room. Jennifer was standing above me. She was wearing tight white pants and a turquoise blouse that had been tied in a knot in front to expose her stomach. A stomach that was flat and, somehow, tanned. She was barefoot and wore a turquoise ribbon in her hair.

"Let's go," she said. "Barnaby just called. He wants us to come up for a drink."

I sat up slowly, fuzzy-headed. "What time is it?"

"Ten o'clock," Jennifer said. "Why don't you take a shower? You've got time. I've got to make a few phone calls."

"Who are you going to call?"

"My boss, for one. To tell him I won't be working this week."

"But it's only seven o'clock in the morning in San Francisco."

"I know, silly. But it's better that way. If he were awake when I called, he might try to talk me into coming back."

I moved slowly toward the bathroom.

"Do you know what I forgot last night?" she called after me. "In all the rush? My grass. Do you have any?"

"Your what?"

"My grass. You know—grass."

"That's okay. We can manage."

"You mean you have some?"

"No. I don't smoke it. I'd rather drink."

"That's all right," Jennifer said cheerfully. "I'll call Patsy and have her put some in the mail."

"Who's Patsy?"

"My roommate. Didn't I tell you about her yesterday? Oh God, what a great kid. Honestly, living with her has been one of the great experiences of my life."

I nodded. Then I realized I had gone around the corner into the bedroom and Jennifer could not see me.

"She bought some stuff last week that she says is pure dynamite. I haven't had a chance to try it yet but I'll have her send us plenty. Do you think Barnaby smokes?"

"I don't know. Listen, I'm going to get in the shower."

41

"I'll have her send enough for three. If he doesn't smoke—wow—we can take some really heavy trips."

I felt old as I went into the bathroom. Jennifer was still talking as I turned the shower on. ". . . Patsy will *die,* simply *die.* She'll be *purple* with envy. She doesn't even know that I met you. She was out last night and all I could do was leave her a note. Oh boy, Pats, now for the gory details . . ."

I drank champagne in Barnaby Blaine's room until I felt all right again. Then we went to the beach. Blaine bought a quart of Scotch and a case of beer for a picnic. While he was in the liquor store I called my publisher from a phone booth. I said I needed $2,000 cash by Monday morning. He said he would arrange it care of the First National Bank of Miami. Things are simple when your book is number one.

We drove along junky Route One in South Miami, and Blaine bought two pounds of spareribs with extra sauce, six ears of corn wrapped in tinfoil, and four bags of French-fried potatoes. I opened beers for all of us as we headed toward the beach. We had the top down and the noon sun beat hard on our heads. There were soft white clouds scattered through the sky and the wind was starting to blow. Blaine drove fast, swerving from lane to lane to beat traffic.

The beer was cold and good. It tasted nourishing after the champagne. We drank quickly and I opened a second round. There was a dull buzz in my head, but so many pleasant sensations: the warmth of Jennifer's thigh next to mine; the coldness and wetness of the beer can in my hand; the heat of the sun and the glare of the day and the cool of the whipping wind. And every pleasure heightened by my knowing I was breaking the rules. I was not supposed to be here, with the top down. In Miami. But for a whole crazy week I'd be safe. Protected from reality by a shield 150 hours thick. Feeling nothing but the joy of wild and sudden fun with strangers. People to whom I owed nothing. Who expected nothing from me except that I enjoy them.

The fears I'd felt earlier—hangover fears—had been dissipated by the champagne. I felt now the way I remembered feeling on Sunday mornings when I would tell my parents I was going to Mass, and after Mass to the beach. I would not go to Mass, of course; I would meet my friends and we would leave with an hour's head start. Driving fast, with the top down, sipping our beers covertly so we would not be noticed by police.

"How about some music?" Blaine shouted over the wind.

"Let me," Jennifer said. "I want to be in charge of the radio."

"It's a deal, sweetheart." He grinned and put a hand on her knee. "That will be your only responsibility of the week."

She looked at me, and then she laughed. "Want to bet?" she shouted. Then she laughed again—a little too loudly, I thought—and buried her face in my neck.

We drove for twenty miles to a beach that Blaine knew.

The sun stayed strong and the wind grew stronger. Jennifer's hair blew madly into my face.

"Are you sure you don't mind this?" I said. "The wind in your hair?"

"Are you kidding? This is what long hair is *for*."

The song on the radio was called "No Time." It was one of the big hits of the month.

> Seasons change, and so do I
> No time left for you,
> No time left for you.

The song made me think of my wife.

Jennifer took her clothes off as soon as we parked the car. Her bikini was tiny and pink. All of her was tanned, except for the tops of her breasts. "Sunlamp and tinfoil," she said. "Six nights a week." The wind was blowing hard and the parking lot was empty. The sun made everything seem bleached. Jennifer paraded around the car in her bikini, kicking her legs and clapping her hands and singing "Let the Sun Shine In" while Blaine and I unloaded picnic supplies.

The beach was called Cape Florida and it was part of a state park. Miles and miles of unbroken white sand and green ocean. And, as far as we could see, deserted. There were whitecaps on the water from the wind. And rich cottony cumulus clouds on the horizon. "Come on," Jennifer said. "Everybody sing: 'Let the sun shine in. Let the sun shine in . . .'" We put the food at the base of a pine tree, in the shade, and then we walked toward the water, inhaling deeply the light, clean air, feeling the hot sand beneath our feet.

Jennifer went swimming right away. For ten minutes she swam straight out, against the waves. Then she turned, in a wide arc, and swam back. Blaine and I, in our bathing suits, stood at the edge of the water and watched. She came out sparkling, and not even out of breath. "It's fantastic," she said. "Let's have races."

Instead we lay on the blankets that Blaine had brought from his room. Jennifer put sun lotion on both of us. She warned us to be careful because the sun was strong and we were pale. Yes, Jennifer, we said, and closed our eyes. She swam again. One hundred breaststrokes, 100 backstrokes, and 300 crawl strokes, without pausing for a rest. That was her daily routine in San Francisco. Then she did a series of underwater tricks that involved holding her breath for forty-five seconds. A good pair of lungs was essential, she said, to the kind of life she planned to lead.

When the sun got too hot, I went up to the pine trees to get beer. Blaine drank Scotch, and we watched Jennifer in the distance. The beer made me full, so I laid the can in the sand and poured Scotch instead. It tasted like honey: rich and sweet.

"Some broad," Blaine said.

"Yeah. Jesus, I don't know if I can keep up with her for a week."

"How long have you known her?"

"Let's see—what time is it now in San Francisco?"

"Huh?"

"I met her at ten o'clock yesterday morning."

"You're kidding."

"She came to my hotel room to interview me for a story."

"I don't believe it."

"And here we are."

"You mean that broad got into the plane and flew to Florida with you and you only met her yesterday morning?"

"Yup."

"She must be nuts."

"No. I don't think so. Just high-spirited is all."

"And you, you idiot. You must be out of your skull."

"What do you mean?"

"Fly a broad all the way across the country to spend a week with you at the race track, and you don't even know her, for Christ's sake?" Blaine stood and began to pace in circles in the sand. "Suppose you don't like her. Or she don't like you? That broad is here for a *week*."

I shrugged. "Look, I didn't plan this. It just happened. But I'm sure it will work out all right."

"Jesus Christ," he said, talking to himself now, and staring at Jennifer, who waved to him from the surf. "What have I done? Twelve years I've been away. Twelve years to get back to Hialeah. And I come back with a couple of nuts."

"Barnaby. We're not nuts."

"No? It's not nuts to sign up to spend a whole week with a broad you don't even know?"

"No. It's not nuts. It's just the new morality."

He laughed again. Then he sat down and poured himself more Scotch. "Well, cheers, kid. Here's to the new morality."

"And," I said, "here's to a profitable week."

We stayed at the beach all afternoon. Eventually Blaine and I swam. Then I rubbed sun lotion on Jennifer's back. Her skin was smooth, and there were blond hairs near the bottom of her spine. She made soft, cooing noises as I rubbed. Blaine sat next to us, silent and contemplative, like an Indian, his legs crossed at the ankles, cradling the bottle of Scotch. We all were drinking Scotch now, and soon it was three-quarters gone. Then I carried the food down and we ate our lunch in the sun. We ate all the ribs, and the corn, but the potatoes were soggy, so we threw them away. The wind was very strong now, and when we tried to pour extra sauce on the ribs, it blew and spattered the blankets and the sand. We giggled, and glowed with the Scotch.

I took Jennifer for a walk after lunch. Blaine fell asleep beneath the pine trees. Jennifer, for once, did not have much to say. We walked along the edge of the water, holding hands. The water was very green and the afternoon was turning cooler in the wind.

"All the colors," I said, "they're so bright." And they were. Green water, blue sky, white sand, orange sun. All of them very intense.

"I'm happy," Jennifer said.

"Good. That's what I want you to be."

"Sometimes I get very depressed."

"About what?"

"The aimlessness of most people's lives. Even though I've brought such order into mine, I get depressed when I see how many people around me seem so lost."

"Well, don't get depressed this week."

She squeezed my hand. "Oh, don't worry. This week is a dream come true."

We walked awhile longer in silence. Then she said, "Do you think it's unreal?"

"What? Us being here?"

"Yes."

"Kind of. Why?"

"That's something else that depresses me. Every time people have fun, they think whatever they're doing is unreal."

"But this is."

"No. This is something that matters. This is a genuine life-experience. We only think it's unreal because it's fun. I hate that. I hate being conditioned to respond that way. Why does this have to be unreal? And what does unreal mean?"

"What you just said. It means a dream. That's what this is. We don't belong here. We can't stay. This is one crazy week of our lives."

"No! I won't accept that. Suppose this is reality. Suppose it's everything else that's unreal. Why can't you think of it that way?"

"I don't know. Because that's not how it is."

"It's whatever way you make it in your mind. I think reality should be our servant. I don't think we should be reality's slaves."

I nodded, even though I had no idea what she meant.

"I'm happy," she said. "And I refuse to say every time that I'm happy, that whatever I'm doing is unreal. That only my depressions are for real."

"Okay. Don't say it."

"Kiss me."

"What?"

"I want you to kiss me. And to press your body close to mine."

She came so close to me, I could smell the salt on her skin. When she looked up at me she seemed like a Mormon pioneer woman who had just laid eyes on the promised land. My head felt orange as the sun. I kissed her. For a long time, with the cool water breaking over our feet. And I pressed my body close.

"Mmmm," she said. "That's what I needed to make it real."

Jennifer went for one more swim before we left. By then the air was cool, the water cold. Even standing in the sun, I got goosebumps as the wind blew hard across my chest. Blaine lay unconscious beneath his blanket in the shade.

I watched her plunge ahead, into the gale and the freezing green. She swam for ten minutes, out against the waves and back. I watched her walk up the beach when she was through. The sun still bright, the water still green, and her pink bathing suit shining against the background of white sand. I felt excitement as I watched her—her body, which really was a lovely body, and her long, wet hair, and the grin on her face and the life inside

49

her. When she got to me I wrapped her in a big towel and kissed her and handed her more Scotch. We dozed in each other's arms while Blaine drove back to the hotel.

It was after seven o'clock when we got there. Dark outside and time for dinner. We still were wobbling a little bit from the Scotch. Two steps inside the living room of the suite I turned Jennifer around by the shoulders and pulled her toward me. Our skins felt sandy when they touched. The air conditioning was sharp against my sunburn. I kissed her hard and slid my hand inside the back of her bikini bottom.

She pushed away from me and stepped backward. Three steps. Until she was just out of reach.

"Do you know what? I got sexually excited once just watching you on television."

"What?"

"With William Buckley. Every time you outsmarted him I tingled in a very special place."

"I didn't outsmart him very often."

"Often enough. We were watching the show at home. Just Patsy and me. I said God, Patsy, God, he's turning me on. But she didn't feel it at all. I guess maybe because she's a conservative."

"Well, they are much harder to arouse."

"I said right then, if I can ever get to meet him, I know something special will happen."

"I think it should happen right now." I stepped forward and pulled her toward me. She resisted. "No, no, not now. Now we're too tired and groggy. And besides, we have to

50

eat. But later, after dinner. When we don't have to worry about time."

Suddenly she trembled in my arms. "It's going to be so special," she said. "It's going to be so special that it scares me. It's so important that everything go just right."

She walked away from me and paused at the bedroom doorway. "I'm going to take a quick shower. Just to wash the sand off. Then we can have our first dinner together in Miami. You can ply me with good conversation and wine. And later we can come back up here."

She had a new and peculiar light in her eye and she was talking loud and very fast. "You can have me then. You can get from me exactly what you want." With an abrupt motion she reached behind her back and unhooked the top of her bikini. She removed it and tossed it on the rug. "Look," she said. "Look at my breasts." They were firm and white, with big nipples. I could see the nipples starting to get hard.

She turned and ran into the bathroom. A moment later I heard the shower start.

Toward the end of dinner I excused myself and went to call my wife. I used a pay phone at the edge of the lobby closest to the salt-water pool. The air blew through an open doorway, slightly damp. The lobby was enormous, and deserted. Very few people wanted to stay in Miami when for the same money they could have Miami Beach.

"Hello?"

"Hello."

There was a moment of silence. I never could think of anything to say to her. Especially on the phone.

"You sound far away," she said.

"I am."

We talked about the kids for a while. And my tour. Then she asked me how the weather was.

"Terrific. Sunny today and in the eighties."

"In San Francisco?"

"I'm not in San Francisco."

"You're not?"

"I'm in Miami."

There was a long silence. The long silences were just about the worst part of our relationship.

When she spoke, it was in a soft, defeated voice: "What about tomorrow?"

"Tomorrow?"

"Are you still coming home?"

"No. I'm afraid I'll be tied up down here all week."

Another silence. Then: "Oh."

"Look, I know you're not happy about this, but something very important has come up."

"Of course."

"What?"

"Of course something important has come up. Something important is always coming up. Because everything else these days is important . . ."

"That's not true."

"We need you here."

"I know, I know. And you'll have me. I promise. In one more week."

There was another silence that threatened to get long. "Aren't you going to ask me why I'm here?"

"No."

"Why not?"

"Because I don't care any more."

"Now look. Try to be reasonable. After four months, one more week is not going to make any difference."

"That's for sure."

"What?"

"I said that's for sure. No difference at all."

And she hung up. Without even asking me what hotel I was at.

When I got back to the table, Jennifer was gone. Blaine was drinking Irish coffee and humming little songs. We had eaten in a French restaurant in the hotel. The food had been terrible, and grossly overpriced even for southern Florida, but all of us had been too drunk to mind it. Martinis before we ate and two bottles of wine with the meal. At $17.50 per bottle, but the whole thing was taken care of by my credit card. All of us were drunk, but Jennifer was drunkest. She had been drinking her wine so fast she had wound up pouring it herself.

"Hey," Blaine said. "I got to tell you something." I noticed that he was mumbling and wondered if that meant I was mumbling, too. "That broad is scared to death."

"Jennifer?"

He nodded. And burped. "About going to bed with you."

"What?"

"As soon as you leave the table, she starts: 'I can't go through with it, I can't go through with it.' She's squeezing my hand black and blue. I said you should've thought of that last night, baby, before you got on the plane."

"But what's she afraid of?"

" 'There's so much at stake,' she tells me. 'There's so much at stake.' I said you're not a virgin, what's the big deal? She says this is much more important than sex. Then she starts blabbering something about her personal moment of truth."

"She's just drunk," I said. "And excited."

She came back to the table and drank two Irish coffees and a brandy. Her eyes were glazed and she had trouble trying to talk. "Come upstairs, Barnaby," she kept saying. "Come back upstairs with us for a drink."

He smiled. I couldn't tell if it was with kindness, or cruelty, or both. "Sorry, sweetheart. I'm exhausted." He rose suddenly, and walked unsteadily toward the lobby.

"Jennifer," I said. "I think it's time to go to bed."


"I'd like a drink," she said.

She was standing in the middle of the room, her legs slightly spread, swaying. I poured her about two inches of Scotch in a glass. Then I got a beer from the refrigerator for myself.

"Are you trying to tell me something?"

"What?"

"I said are you trying to tell me something?" She was holding her glass at arm's length. Her grip did not seem strong.

"I don't understand you."

"How come I didn't get a full drink?"

"The bottle's right there. If you want more you can pour it yourself."

"No. I want you to pour it for me. And fill it. To the top."

I looked at her for a long time. Then I said quietly, "Jennifer, I think you've had enough."

"I know I've had enough. That's not the point." She was starting to raise her voice. "Don't you understand anything?" Suddenly she pivoted, yelled "*Shit!*" and smashed her glass against a wall. Then she ran into the bedroom and slammed the door. Then I heard her crying.

I sat on the couch with my beer, lit a cigarette, and looked out the window at the bay. Clouds had come in and there wasn't any moon. If I had skipped the Irish coffee after dinner, I might have been able to think more clearly of what to do. But I couldn't think of anything, so I decided to sit on the couch and wait.

The crying stopped. For five minutes there was silence and I thought she had fallen asleep. Then I heard the bathroom water run. She opened the door and walked across the room and sat down next to me and put her arms around me and her face next to mine and I kissed her, hard and long, and our tongues began to move and by the time I took my mouth away she was lying on her back on the couch and I was lying on top of her and I had one hand underneath her pink polka-dot dress.

"I'm sorry," she whispered, and pulled my head back to her and we kissed again and this time when we stopped I had my hand a little further.

I sat up, breathing hard. "Don't worry about it," I said. "Do you think I could have a drink?"

"Sure."

I got up and made her a Scotch, filling the short glass to the brim. I also got another beer for myself. I sat next to her on the couch and put my arm around her.

"It's so confusing," she said.

"Barnaby told me at dinner you were scared."

"I was."

"There's nothing to be scared of, you know. There isn't any pressure."

"Hah."

"There isn't. I'm serious. If you'd be more comfortable tonight, I could sleep out here. I can sleep out here all week. This isn't any sort of a trap. I just want you to have fun."

She was laughing. She threw her head back and poured half the glass of Scotch down her throat and then she laughed again. Louder.

"What's so funny?"

"You really don't understand. You don't understand a damned thing."

"What don't I understand?"

But she only started to laugh again, and then, in the middle of it, suddenly she was crying. She brought herself under control and reached for a cigarette. Then she finished her drink. That was three ounces of Scotch and it had gone in five minutes. On top of everything else she had drunk all day and night. She threw the cigarette, still lit, onto the carpet and plunged her head into my lap and started to push her face into my groin.

I sat her up. "Jennifer, what's wrong with you?"

She was crying again, and said "Shit-shit-shit-shit-shit" between sobs. "Don't you know what I'm afraid of?"

"No, goddamnit, I have no idea."

"I'm afraid of you. Of what you are. You're not just another new guy in my life—you're somebody famous. You've written a book. I've seen you on television. You've actually experienced so much of what I dream about. I mean . . . you're on a first-name basis with . . . with some of the biggest celebrities of our time."

"So, big deal."

"It *is* a big deal. It's given you an aura. And that's what I'm afraid of. Of exposing myself to that aura."

"Jesus Christ, the cigarette!"

It had burned a hole in the carpet and now the carpet itself was starting to smolder. I stamped it out with my shoe. "Go ahead, I didn't mean to interrupt."

"I need another drink."

"A small one."

"A small one would be fine."

She put her head in her hands and rubbed her eyes. I came back with the drink. She took one sip and suddenly started to cry again and lunged forward, spilling the drink, which she had set on her lap, and throwing her arms around me and kissing me frantically all over my face.

"Don't you know what I'm after? Don't you know what I want? A real relationship. With you. I want to mean something to you. I want you, with all your fame and success, to care about *me*."

The Scotch had made a big stain on her dress and was all over her legs, but she did not seem to feel it.

"Jennifer," I said, "let's go to bed."

While I was in the bathroom I could hear her bumping around the walk-in closet. I came out, wearing only pants, and found her squatting in front of her giant garment bag, trying to untie a knot.

"What are you doing?"

"Trying to open this."

"What for?"

"To get my nightgown out."

"Do you really think you'll need a nightgown?"

"I need this nightgown. It's very important. And I can't"—she started pulling the garment bag, trying to tear it open—"get this damned"—she was starting to cry again, too, and then, losing her balance, she fell over on her side—"knot out!"

"Wait a minute." I went back to the bathroom and took a razor blade from a dispenser I had on top of the sink. I bent down and cut the strap with the blade. Then I stood and unzipped the bag.

"Get your nightgown," I said. "I'll be in bed."

I took off my pants and got into the double bed closer to the bathroom. A minute later Jennifer walked past, into the bathroom, without looking at me, carrying something white. While she was in the bathroom, I got out of bed and turned off the light. I got back and she came out of the bathroom, leaving the light on behind her. Instead of getting into bed, she walked across the room and turned the bedroom light back on.

"What's the point of wearing this nightgown if the lights are out?" she said. Then she walked back and turned off the bathroom light.

The nightgown was long and white and had a high collar and lacy red trim down the front. It was heavy enough so I could barely make out the outline of her body underneath. Not counting flannels, it was one of the least provocative nightgowns I had ever seen.

"Isn't it beautiful?" Jennifer said, and stood before me, waiting to be admired.

"It's nice, Jennifer. It's nice."

"It's more than nice. It's beautiful. And guess where I got it."

"I have no idea."

"Come on, guess. Guess who gave it to me."

"Your boss at work."

"No, guess seriously."

"Jennifer, I don't know. I don't even know anyone else you know. How am I supposed to guess?"

"Come on, try at least. It'll really be a surprise."

"William Buckley."

For a minute I thought she was going to cry again. Instead, she stopped smiling, walked around the bed, got in, and said, "My brothers."

"Your brothers?"

"Yes, my two younger brothers. They're nineteen and seventeen and they gave it to me for Christmas. Isn't that

59

groovy? Isn't that just the grooviest thing you can imagine? I love them for doing that. It's so wonderful to find out that your kid brothers recognize that you're a woman. Our family is so great that way. We have no inhibitions at all."

"That's terrific, Jennifer. That's really terrific. And it's one heck of a piece of apparel. Now would you like me to turn out the light?"

"Not unless you're ready to go to sleep."

"Not quite."

"I want you to make love to me."

"I want to make love to you. And I intend to make love to you. Now. That's why I was going to turn out the light."

"No. I hate to make love in the dark. You might as well be an alley cat, making love in the dark. I like to make love with the lights on. That makes me feel like a woman."

"Okay. So we'll make love with the lights on."

She got up on her knees on the bed. Smiling now, but not at me. At the bay and the clouds beyond the window. "All right," she said. Holding her hands over her head.

"What?"

"I'm ready. You can slide the nightgown gently over my head."

I did, and she took it from my hands. She folded it solemnly, as a Boy Scout would the American flag. Then she laid it on the floor beside the bed. We were both on our knees, naked and three feet apart.

"This was how we started on New Zealand," Jennifer said. "On our knees. I think it adds a spiritual dimension."

Then she lunged at me, as if she were tackling a quarterback, and we had intercourse all over the king-sized bed with the lights on.

Much later, when we had finished, she got out of the bed, put her nightgown back on, turned out the light, and climbed into the bed by the window.

"What are you doing?" I whispered in the dark.

"Going to sleep."

"Well, come here. Sleep here."

"I can't."

"Why not?"

"I can't sleep in a bed with anyone else. I don't get the proper amount of rest."

"Jennifer, that's ridiculous!"

"Ssssh. Go to sleep."

"Jennifer!"

"Good night. That was beautiful. I feel very much at peace with myself."

# Monday

BARNABY BLAINE *was shaved and dressed at*
*5:05* A.M. *He walked quickly along the deserted cor-*
*ridor outside his room and rode the silent, carpeted*
*elevator to the lobby. Then he walked out the front*
*door of the hotel, past a doorman sleeping in the*
*valet parking booth. The predawn air was damp, the*
*sky swollen with clouds, the streets deserted. Blaine*
*made a right turn in front of the hotel, crossed a*
*small drawbridge over a canal, and continued a mile*
*and a half, past neatly trimmed shrubbery, to down-*
*town Miami. From twelve years before he remem-*

62

*bered the newsstand, at Second and Flagler, to which
the* Morning Telegraph *was delivered. Once, along
the way, a patrol car paused and its two tired inhabi-
tants asked where he was going. He showed them his
room key and they drove off.*

*The newsstand was still there, but closed. Alone
among fluorescent streetlights, Blaine rooted among
stacks of Miami* Heralds *and out-of-town papers like
the* New York Times *and* Wall Street Journal *until he
found the neat, bound bundle that he wanted. With a
penknife that he had carried in his pocket for that
purpose, he cut the string, removed three papers, and
left $2.25 in quarters and dimes stacked neatly on top
of a front-page* Herald *picture of a rock singer who
had been arrested for indecent exposure during a performance in Miami the night before.*

*He walked back to his room, the sky lighter now,
but gray. Once inside, he placed two of the* Morning
Telegraphs, *unopened, on an end table by the couch.
With practiced hand he turned the pages of the third
until he came to the section he wanted: past performance records of horses running that day at Hialeah.
He laid the paper on the bar and stared at it, waiting
for his mind to click on. His elbows rested on the bar;
he supported his face with clenched fists. There was a
faint, sour odor to his breath. Almost immediately, as
though chemically triggered by the newsprint, his
brain began to work. Once started, it functioned
automatically, like an electric generator that emitted
a low and constant hum.*

*The first at Hialeah. One mile and an eighth, for*

*fillies and mares, four years old and up. Claiming price, $3,500. That meant for $3,500 any registered owner on the grounds could buy any of the horses in the race. Which meant none of these horses was worth a damn, because no owner would risk losing a good horse for that price. At Hialeah, Blaine knew, $3,500 claiming horses were as cheap as they came. And these were females besides. Trying to go a mile and an eighth, which, these days, was considered a distance race. Cheap females, Blaine knew, could not be counted on to stay the route. He chuckled without pleasure as the thought occurred that the truth of that axiom extended beyond the borders of the race track. Smiling, he turned the page. One of those horses would win the first race, but there was no reliable way to determine in advance which one. Which meant none of Barnaby Blaine's money would be risked.*

*The second at Hialeah. Six furlongs—three-quarters of a mile. For four-year-olds and up of either sex. Claiming price, $7,500. Still cheap, but considerably better grade than the first race. And running a shorter, less troublesome distance. Blaine inserted a cigar in his mouth and lit it. Leaving the paper where it was, he went to his suitcases and began to unpack and organize his equipment. Loose-leaf binders, hundreds of pages thick. Graphs and charts, and files of index cards in metal boxes. Two slide rules, a well-traveled adding machine, and one large wooden-handled magnifying glass. It took him twenty minutes to get ready. Then, holding a ballpoint pen in his* *hand, he began to examine the record of the first horse in the race. It had not run since the previous November. Cheap horses were bad bets after layoffs; there was no accurate guide to their condition. Proceeding no further, Blaine drew a large X through the horse's name. His hand trembled slightly and the X was drawn with wavering lines.*

———————

Jennifer was standing over me, naked and rumpled, grinning and warm.

"Come on," she said. "The water's just right."

I heard the shower running and saw steam drifting out of the bathroom. "What time is it?"

"Seven-fifteen. Come on, I want to lather you up from head to toe."

"Jennifer. Are you serious? Seven-fifteen?"

"It's the latest I've slept in weeks." She reached down and pulled me by the hand. "Let's go. There's nothing more romantic than bathing together."

"But this is a shower."

"More hygienic. Come on." She tugged.

I yielded to a sitting position. "I think I'm sick. I think I need more sleep." I felt rudely awakened and betrayed. Betrayed because I remembered drinking Scotch, and you were not supposed to get this kind of a hangover from drinking Scotch. But then, slowly groping their way through my mind like the survivors of a plane crash, came memories of the drinks that had preceded and followed the Scotch.

"I had much more to drink than you did," Jennifer said.

"And I feel great." She let go of my hand, pivoted, and touched her toes five times. Then she started to do knee bends.

"Okay, okay," I said. "I get the picture."

She was very thorough about her shower, as if she were demonstrating to a physical education class. She lathered me up from head to toe, as promised, and scrubbed at my genitals as if she were trying to cure a venereal disease. I reciprocated, although in my condition I found the whole business as romantic as washing a car.

But she loved it. She bubbled away, talking and humming, telling me how quickly she was learning to like and admire Barnaby Blaine and how wonderful it was that the three of us had found each other, because, obviously, each had so much to contribute to the other's lives. There was something magical about us as a unit, she said; she had felt it on the beach. Something that made our whole greater than the sum of our parts.

When finally I had got her covered with soap, she moved to the back of the tub and faced the hot, strong spray. She lifted her right leg until it was perpendicular to her waist, as if she were punting a football. Then she held it there and counted slowly to twenty, saying "hippopotamus" between the numbers. "One hippopotamus, two hippopotamus . . . eleven hippopotamus . . . seventeen hippopotamus . . ." Then she did the same with her left leg. I watched in silence, crowded into the other end of the tub.

"Time is so precious," she said when she was done. "I simply have to exercise. And I have to get clean. Isn't it wonderful there's a way to do both at once?"

She stepped forward, rinsed the rest of herself, and reached for the faucets. "Okay. Ready for the cold?"

"*No!*"

"Sure you are." She twisted the hot water all the way off and the cold all the way on. I lunged past her and broke two rings from the curtain getting out. She sang an operatic note and held it for twenty seconds as I wiped steam from the mirror and looked inside. I was pale, my beard stubble cancerous and black, my hair getting thin, my eyes red and puffy, my stomach soft and no longer flat.

Jennifer shut off the water. Threw back the curtain and jumped glowing and pink from the tub. "*Chicken!*" she said, and made a face. If she had been holding a towel, I believe she would have snapped it at me.

We tried breakfast in the hotel coffee shop, but Jennifer would not eat. She said all she ate for breakfast was fresh fruit. The hotel had plenty of fresh fruit—oranges, grapefruit, bananas, pineapple, even papaya—but Jennifer said hotels kept their fruit fresh with chemical injections and that she would eat only fresh fruit that came from an outdoor market. It seemed strange that someone who the night before had drunk so freely of Scotch that had been preserved for twelve years now insisted that her oranges be no more than twelve hours off the tree. But it was Monday morning, the sun was starting to burn through the overcast, it was my first day at Hialeah with my exuberant new girl friend and the racing expert who was going to make me rich. Even hung over, I was not in any mood for a quarrel.

We went downtown in a cab, in search of fresh fruit.

Jennifer brought along a notebook, saying she might interview some Cuban refugees and ask them how they liked Miami. Then she would write a story and send it to the manager of The Dream Team in New York as an example of her initiative.

We bought two oranges from a cart in front of a delicatessen. Speaking Spanish, Jennifer asked the proprietor if he longed to return to his homeland and whether or not he thought Castro was mistreating any of the relatives he'd left behind.

The proprietor, however, turned out to be an Italian from the Bensonhurst section of Brooklyn.

"Careful," Barnaby Blaine said as he answered our knock on his door. "Watch where you walk."

It was ten-thirty in the morning. Newspapers covered his floor. All of the thirty *Morning Telegraphs* he had brought from San Francisco had been opened to the Hialeah section and spread across his rug. Thin trails of blue carpet wound among them. Along one of these Blaine stepped slowly, with great care, his arms extended to either side for balance. It was as if he were tiptoeing through a flower bed—or a minefield.

Jennifer and I followed, moving stealthily, like Indians. Jennifer giggled. Blaine turned quickly and gave her a sharp look. We tiptoed to the bar at the other end of the room, where Blaine motioned toward vacant stools on which we could sit.

"I'm almost finished," he said. "I've only got the tenth race to do."

Along the length of the bar I saw a dozen loose-leaf notebooks, each opened to a page containing a graph. There were line graphs, bar graphs, circle graphs; points plotted in red ink and black ink and green. Also on the bar were two slide rules, a small adding machine, stacks of different-colored index cards—orange, turquoise, pink— all blank and unlined, and one large wooden-handled magnifying glass.

Blaine turned a few pages of the bar graph book, and then made a calculation on the slide rule. As he worked, he sipped absently from a cup of coffee that looked as if it had been left by the guest who had occupied the room before him. After a few minutes he tapped out some numbers on the adding machine and began to print letters and numbers on one of the turquoise cards.

I had not the slightest idea what he was doing, although I presumed it related, in some way, to the racing we would witness that afternoon.

"What does it mean?" Jennifer whispered.

"It's complicated," I whispered back. "I'll explain later."

Blaine began chuckling to himself, then gathered a batch of orange and pink and turquoise cards together, secured them into a packet, and bound it with a rubber band. Then he got up from his stool, moved quickly along one of the paths of blue to a point halfway to the door, crouched, gazed through his magnifying glass for a moment, muttered something unintelligible, and returned to the bar, where he began working again with the slide rule.

"Can you imagine?" Jennifer whispered. "If this is what

it's like to pick horse races, can you imagine what a National Security Council meeting must be like?"

Ten minutes later Blaine finished. He drank the last of his cold coffee and smiled. "You slept well?" he said.

"Terrific," Jennifer said. "Terrific. And guess what? I'm not frightened any more."

"I'm delighted," Blaine said.

"How does it look today?" I said. "You see anything you like?"

"Always. Always I see something I like. The question is how much do I like it. And does the potential return justify the risk of investment. These answers are not found in hotel rooms. So if you'll allow me to wash my face and put on a fresh shirt, we can make our debut at the race course."

"Already?" Jennifer said.

Blaine smiled. "Remember, sweetheart? That's why we're here."

"But I thought the racing didn't start until afternoon. I was just getting ready to go swimming."

Blaine shook his head. "A late start," he said, "is the devil's workshop. I always arrive at the track before noon. Besides, this is Hialeah. Remember? An old girl friend of mine. The least I can do after all these years is meet her for lunch."

Barnaby Blaine was such an expert that he did not even bring his *Morning Telegraph* to the race track. He handed Jennifer and me our copies, unopened and fresh, but refolded his own used edition and left it on the bar. He said he had spent four and a half hours making his calcula-

tions in the privacy and calm of his room; there was no
sense bringing the paper to the track and maybe deciding
to revise them amid the pressures and temptations of the
afternoon. "Besides," he said, "there's something so—
sticky—about a *Telegraph* that's been used. To bring it
with you to the track is like going unshaven."

Jennifer giggled when he said this and started writing
in her stenographer's notebook. Writing with the ballpoint
pen that had a plastic daisy in one end. She said she was
planning a story on Barnaby Blaine for The Dream Team.
About how he was one guy who really did beat the races.
She thought if she wrote about so unlikely a subject as
that, the manager of The Dream Team would be im-
pressed with her versatility.

"I have a question," Jennifer said. "What do you do at
the race track between races? When you're by yourself,
with nobody to talk to?"

"I read. Last year at Santa Anita, I read *Ulysses* and
*Remembrance of Things Past*. Three summers ago at
Hollywood Park, I got through the entire Old Testament.
And I only had two losing days that whole meeting."

We stopped at the bank on the way to the track. My
$2,000 was waiting. The sun had come out strongly and
the sky was clear. Blaine put the top down and drove in
the left lane of the expressway. He wore a seersucker
sports jacket and smoked a long, thin cigar. A pair of
expensive Japanese binoculars in a glossy leather case lay
beside him on the seat. Jennifer sat close to me, squeezing

71

my hand and occasionally blowing warm breath in my ear.

"I'm trying to distract you," she said. "Am I distracting you?"

"A little bit." Actually, she was not distracting me at all. I just wanted to get to the track. All I could think about was betting horses.

"How much do you think you'll win?" Jennifer asked me.

"Hard to say." My heart was pounding and I could feel my legs starting to tremble. I had $2,000 in my pocket and the first real horse-racing expert I'd ever known was driving the car.

"Just make sure you win enough for your plane fare."

"My plane fare home? I can take care of it with the card. The publisher is paying for that."

She tugged at my earlobe with her hand. "Silly, I don't mean your plane fare home. I mean your plane fare to Salt Lake City. For when you come out to visit."

The white concrete shimmered in the sun. Blaine pushed the red Ford to eighty, and it shuddered. Jennifer found a Joe Cocker song on the radio and turned it up as loud as it would go.

The approach to Hialeah is like the approach to no other race track in America. You get off the expressway at 79th Street and drive down this long boulevard that is lined with rundown houses and stores with Spanish writing in the windows. ("Ooh, refugees," Jennifer said. "Can we stop?") Just as the shabbiness is starting to get you depressed, you turn and you are into the prettiest two hundred acres in Florida.

## The Dream Team

We saw a long row of hedge, ten feet tall. Beyond it were giant palm trees and Australian pines. Blaine crossed an intersection and pulled into a driveway and suddenly the palms were on either side of us: enormous, with round, smooth trunks. Blaine was smiling, but he was squeezing the steering wheel so hard his knuckles were white.

Hialeah's driveway is long and silent. It curves gracefully, like the neck of a beautiful woman. The clubhouse is open and clean. Built of pink stucco and green tile. It looks like the residence of a South American dictator—a benevolent one, friendly to the West. As we drove toward it, through the still-deserted parking lot, I felt like I was the new ambassador arriving to present my credentials, hoping I would be asked to stay for lunch.

"How does it feel," Jennifer asked Blaine, "to be returning here after an absence of so many years?" She had her notebook in her lap and her daisy pen poised.

But Blaine said nothing. His mouth was open slightly, a half-smile on his face, and his eyes were shifting focus continually as he looked at the clubhouse and the race track and infield that lay beyond. It was as if he were viewing a great painting for the first time after having admired prints of it for years.

We paid our admission at the clubhouse gate and bought our programs. The picture on the cover was of a portion of the island that lay in the infield lake. There were two tall palm trees with a herd of flamingos at their base. Half a dozen flamingos, their necks craned forward, their wings outstretched in full flight, glided gently through the air past the leafy tops of the trees. In the background were pine trees and a turquoise sky, the color of Blaine's index cards.

We walked through the green-floored clubhouse lobby, strangely empty on a Monday at noon, our heels echoing on the tile. We walked past the barber shop and the souvenir stand where they sold Hialeah sunglasses, cigarette lighters, key rings, jewelry, and binoculars, and rode up the escalator to the top level, where we would have an unobstructed view of the races all afternoon.

"It's beautiful!" Jennifer said.

For once, the exclamation points she spoke in were appropriate. The track itself was a broad, neatly raked band of light brown dirt; beyond it was the infield. First the turf course, where the grass races were run. Lush, green, closely cropped golf-course grass, almost glinting beneath the sun. There was no element of the sport more lovely than watching through a good pair of binoculars the brightly colored silks of the jockeys in a closely packed field as they came around the homestretch turn in a grass race. The green background magically transforming the scene from a sporting event into an image that lingered in the mind like art.

Behind the turf course was the totalisator board, a long, low strip of electricity whose beauty, cold and stark, lay in its impersonal efficiency. Hundreds of thousands of dollars, representing the perceptions, intuitions, and hopes of thousands of human beings were digested by the pari-mutuel machines, and their disposition flashed minute-by-minute by the winking electric numbers on this board. The odds, brought up to date every ninety seconds before the race, defined the parameters of one's dreams. The order of finish, flashed ruthlessly and without comment, within moments of the running, was judge, jury, and appeals court. The shame of one's defeat, the glory of a more infrequent triumph were proclaimed impartially for all to see. There was an inescapable permanence to those numbers. Once the red "Official" sign flashed on, the last hope for clemency was ground to dust. No phone call from the governor could bring redemption. The 8–5 horse who could not lose but did was now part of the permanent record. A statistic, and a statistic only, for the Barnaby Blaines of the nation to reflect upon.

The totalisator board. In the age of the machine, the age of the computer, there was no better example of the omnipotent, soulless power that man had wrought. To which thousands came daily, to pay obeisance and beg favor, unable to believe that there were nothing but transistors at the core.

The presence of the infield lake was thus not only welcome, but almost necessary. Man-made also, but born of a gentler impulse. The lake was occupied by an island, and during racing season at least, by a Seminole Indian in a canoe. The island was occupied, year-round, by the world's largest captive herd of flamingos: the garish pink hub of the track. If their coloring had not been natural, a local chamber of commerce undoubtedly would have painted them. But it was natural—a pink that glowed in the dark. A pink that had become the symbol of Hialeah.

The walls of the race track, even in the grandstand, were painted flamingo-pink; the richest race was the Flamingo Stakes, and in the grandstand there was even a tame flamingo, which, for a dollar, would pose for a picture with a visitor.

From a distance, clustered together on the island in the heat of the midday sun, the five hundred or so flamingos looked like the biggest pink chrysanthemum in the world. Occasionally, for no discernible reason, small squadrons of them would leave the main group and trace a long oval pattern in the sky. Later in the day a similar but larger flight would be initiated by the management. After the sixth race each day the Indian poled his dugout canoe slowly across the lake, and as he approached the island on which the birds were sunning themselves, blessedly oblivious to the anguish occurring all around them, he shouted at them and made menacing gestures with his pole. This action, unfailingly, so alarmed the birds that, at a minimum, two-thirds of the herd took sudden and spectacular flight. Then the track announcer, who, incidentally, possessed a voice that was not without birdlike qualities of its own, would say, over the loudspeakers: "Ladies and gentlemen, may we direct your attention to the infield, where the world famous Flight of the Flamingos is about to take place." Then, with all eyes riveted, the birds leapt skyward and a disconcertingly scratchy recording called "Flight of the Flamingos" was played. Whether the recording was intended to encourage the birds or to mollify disgruntled bettors, I never could be sure.

We walked to the grandstand and bought paper plates full of clams on the half-shell. Then Blaine led us into the sunshine, across the neatly trimmed lawn that surrounded the walking ring and led to the paddock. We walked past the tropical bird sanctuary and the tropical fish aquarium, to an open-sided, shaded bar called the Sidewalk Café. Other early arrivals turned to stare as Jennifer walked past. She was radiant in yellow, radiant as the day itself. She noticed the stares she was getting and began to move her hips a little more as she walked. She tried to stop herself from grinning with pleasure, but she could not.

"All right," Blaine said, sipping a seventy-five-cent beer from a false-bottomed mug. "Take out your programs and copy down what I tell you. I want you to know what to bet in case I should suddenly be rendered speechless by a stroke."

"Oh, Barnaby," Jennifer said, and she giggled.

Blaine planned to bet only three horses all day; in the third, ninth, and tenth races. I was starting to understand how he got the Old Testament read at Hollywood Park. I marked the names of the horses in my program but I was uncomfortable with the thought that there would be seven races run that afternoon on which I would not bet.

"Are you sure that's all?"

He looked up sharply from his beer. He wore horn-rimmed bifocals for his work. "What do you mean, am I sure?"

"I mean there's nothing else we can bet?"

"Yes, there's about sixty-five other horses you can bet. But I'm not going to."

"Well, maybe you can tell me who you like in the other races, just in case I decide to bet them."

"Hey, what do you think? That I'm trying to deprive

myself of pleasure? You think that's why I only bet three horses a day? Look, there's going to be a winner in every race. And plenty of people out here are going to bet him. If you try, I hope you succeed. All I'm telling you is after twenty-five years of wrestling with these bastards, the most important lesson I've learned is that the fewer races you bet the better are your chances to make money."

I nodded. I knew he was right. Most days there were only a couple of races where you could tell enough about the horses to be able to make a logical choice. The rest were lotteries. Over the long run, you would do far better confining yourself only to the real races and making much larger, and less frequent, bets. But I was itchy. I had $2,000 and I was in Florida for a week. I didn't know if I could sit still for seven races a day.

With no bet until the third, we had no reason to hurry back to our shaded seats. The sun felt good, and the beer, even at ten cents an ounce, tasted fine. We stayed at the Sidewalk Café and waited patiently for our streak of good fortune to begin.

I still had my *Morning Telegraph* folded in my lap. Fresh, unopened, it was as full of promise as Christmas morning. Only later, when you plunged into the guts of it, into the maze of numbers and abbreviations that had to be cracked like a code, did the glow of that promise start to fade.

But now, I reminded myself, I did not have to bother. Blaine had taken the plunge for us all. Five hours' work in the morning and he had found three horses to bet. There was no point in my looking for more. I reached out for

Jennifer's hand and glanced at the front page of the paper, the page that had the news about the big races of the day all over the country.

The headline stopped me short:

JOIE DE VIVRE FACES SEVEN IN HIALEAH SPRINT

Joie de Vivre. Last year's two-year-old champion. A brilliant colt, unbeaten in eight starts, and what's more, a son of Chateaugay. I got a warm feeling inside me as I read the story. Chateaugay, goddamnit—even after all these years the thrill that horse had given me would not fade. And here was his son now, looking like an even greater horse.

Joie de Vivre's last race had been at Belmont Park in New York last fall, on the Saturday before I started my tour. As a going-away present, my publisher had arranged for a limousine to pick me up at my hotel and take me to the track for the day. Four of us had gone, breakfasting on Guinness Stout and cheese in the back seat. The day had been brilliant: clear blue sky, sharp autumn sun. The feature race had been for two-year-olds, then nearing the end of their first season of racing. The purse had been more than $100,000. I had been losing steadily through the afternoon, but not caring much, because of the Guinness, and later, the race-track beer. Also not caring because the money I was betting was expense-account money the publisher had given me for my tour. I had taken $1,000 to the track and lost $300 by the time of the feature race. And I was just drunk enough to get sentimental about Joie de Vivre.

"He'll win the Derby next year," I told my friends. "Just

like his father did." Then I bored them with the story of my first Derby, with Chateaugay, and I walked to the paddock to watch Joie de Vivre get saddled for the race.

He was chestnut-colored, like Chateaugay, but he seemed taller and more rangy. Over the winter he would fill out, grow stronger, better able to face the tests of weight and distance that his three-year-old season would bring. Now he was mostly speed and promise. Also, I noticed from his charts, he had more than a little bit of heart. Three times in his first seven races he had been leading going into the homestretch, had surrendered the lead to another horse, then had come on again to regain it and win the race. That was a mark of true class, of championship ability, worthy of a son of Chateaugay.

The class would be required the following year, as a three-year-old, when he was entered in the classic events. For now, for this crisp but mellow October afternoon, all he had to do was run the legs off a bunch of other two-year-olds at seven furlongs. There was no reason in the world to think he would not do it. I watched him in the walking ring, watched his jockey, John Rand, one of the best, climb atop him, and then I made my decision. The mixture of beer and sentiment and someone else's money was too much. I went to the $100 window and bought five tickets to win on Joie de Vivre.

For the next fifteen minutes I sat trembling and silent in my seat. I told no one what I had done. If he lost, I never would. If he won, I would casually take the tickets from my pocket and ask one of the girls if she would cash it. A callow kind of fun, but $500 was by far the biggest bet of my life. If I won, I could afford to be callow.

Rand got Joie de Vivre out of the gate first, opened up a lead of three lengths down the backstretch, and then just sat there, holding the horse back, making sure he would have strength in reserve for the stretch. On the turn, a couple of horses drew to within a length, and watching through binoculars, I could see Rand let out the rein. Not hit the horse, not even actively urge him forward. Just loosen the grip enough to say all right, if you'd like to run, you're allowed to.

By the time he had straightened out in the homestretch, Joie de Vivre was four lengths in front. He won by six, with Rand just holding on. He had not been required to show his courage that day; his speed had been enough.

I was hardly the only person at Belmont Park who had thought Joie de Vivre was going to win. He had gone off at odds of 3–5, which meant he returned $3.60 on a $2 bet, and $900 to me. That was a $400 profit, enough to put me ahead for the day. I left the track happy, and the next day took a train to Philadelphia to start my tour.

I had been too busy in the fall to keep up with the racing news, but reading the *Telegraph* now, I learned that Joie de Vivre had come out of that Belmont race slightly sore. Nothing serious, his trainer had explained, but there had been an inflammation of the ankle and it was considered wiser not to risk serious injury by racing him again that year. This meant passing up a $200,000 race in New Jersey, but the prestige of winning the Derby, the Preakness, and the Belmont Stakes the next year was considered more important. Besides, for once, it seemed as if an owner and trainer cared something about the horse itself. "If he's not fit," the trainer was quoted as saying, "he doesn't run. He's fit today, he wintered well, he's come back strong and fresh, he's done everything in his work-outs that we've asked him for, and we're very optimistic about the future."

The six-furlong race this afternoon was a preparation for the Flamingo Stakes, the first important race for the three-year-olds who were aiming for the Kentucky Derby. The Flamingo would be run on Saturday, the last day of our week. So if Joie de Vivre ran well today and came out healthy, I'd be able to watch him run twice. And be able to bet on him twice. For a moment I was tempted not to make any other bets all week. Then I remembered that Joie de Vivre had not been one of the horses Blaine had picked. In fact, Blaine had selected nothing in that race.

"Hey, Barnaby," I said. "Joie de Vivre's running today. How come you didn't pick him?"

"When was his last race, October?"

"Yeah, but he's undefeated."

"And he came out sore?"

"But it says in the paper he's all better."

"One of the first, and least expensive, things I learned about this business is you don't bet a horse his first start of the year."

"But this is a championship horse."

"Was. Last year. Until he proves it again on the track, this year he's just another race horse."

"Oh, come on. I saw him win at Belmont last fall by six lengths."

"What did he pay?"

"Three-sixty."

"That's another thing. Any horse goes off at less than even money, I don't bet."

"Why not?"

"Horses that go off at less than even money win fifty percent of the time. That means they lose fifty percent of the time." Then he explained to Jennifer that even money meant a $2 profit on a $2 bet. "You get less than that, on horses that lose half the time, you're going to lose money in the end. That arithmetic is so simple I don't even need my adding machine."

"Well, I don't care," I said. "Joie de Vivre is an exception."

"Exceptions, in this business, should be avoided. That lesson was a little more expensive."

"I don't want to argue. I'm sure you're right. But I'd better warn you ahead of time, I'm a little bit in love with that horse."

We walked back across the lawn toward our seats, glowing slightly with our optimism and our beer. The horses for the first race were being saddled. We paused by the white fence of the walking ring to watch. Here, again, I was struck by sudden beauty. The aura, even before a cheap race, was impressive. The horses making their stately parade around the white-fenced ring, their coats glistening in the sun. Craggy-faced jockeys, or else jockeys who looked too young to shave, nodding gravely in their brilliant silks as they received riding instructions from their trainers. The wealthy owners and their expensive women, confident and tanned, conversing easily about the things that rich people know. Then the call of "Riders up," and with jockeys aboard, one final trip around the ring. Then the slow processional along the dirt path and through the short tunnel beneath the grandstand, to the track.

In contrast to the measured pace at which the horses walked was the mad scurry toward the betting windows by the hundreds who had waited until they'd seen the horses before they bet.

I felt suddenly proud of myself. I did not have to hurry along with them. I knew this race was not worth betting. Blaine had explained about the cheap females and the distance. I would save my money through this race and the next and make a bet three times as big when a good race came along. I watched the other bettors, who did not know as much as I did, as they strained toward the windows, desperate to get down Daily Double bets. That was another thing Blaine had said: no betting on the Daily Double. A lottery, a gimmick to separate the bettor from his money. I watched the hundreds who did not realize this, watched their tense, joyless faces—it was as if they knew in advance that they would lose, and, indeed, many probably did know, since it had happened so often in the past—and then I looked at Jennifer, walking so blissfully beside me, and at Blaine, so calm, so competent, so assured. Like a pilot entering the cockpit of his plane. For the first time in the fifteen years I had been going to the horse races, I felt superior to the people I saw around me.

I felt no less superior when we lost the third race. I stared briefly at the thin cardboard ticket that had been worth $100 a few moments before, and then I folded it in half and used it to dislodge a piece of clam from beneath my teeth.

Blaine lowered the binoculars through which he had watched the race. He was smiling, just as he had been before it. "One of the sixty percent," he said.

"Ooh," said Jennifer, "too bad."

I shrugged. I felt no disappointment. Blaine had taken great care to explain that even with his methods he lost sixty percent of his bets. The forty percent that he won, however, assured him of profit. I had lost $100, but with $1,900 more in my pocket, and Jennifer at my side, it made no difference. I only wondered how I would be able to resist betting Joie de Vivre.

Blaine pointed out a horse called Sea Change in the sixth race. This was at seven furlongs—seven-eighths of a mile—for two-year-olds, most of whom were nominated for the Flamingo. Sea Change was favorite at 4–5. Less than even money, but except for that, Blaine said, we'd be betting him.

"I want you to watch him," Blaine said, "because not only do I think he'll win today, but I think there's a good chance that he'll run your Joie de Vivre into the ground in the Flamingo."

Sea Change won by four lengths. I watched him canter back to the winner's circle. He did not seem even to be breathing hard. I looked him up in my *Telegraph*. Only two starts as a two-year-old; both wins. The week before he had won a six-furlong race at Hialeah by five lengths.

Then I looked at the top of his chart and saw that his sire was the great European champion Sea Bird.

"He cost $325,000 as a yearling," Blaine said. "And he looks like he's worth every dime."

"He's not as good as Joie de Vivre."

"Don't get emotional. It's much too early to tell. All I'm telling you is that if he isn't any better, he's not much worse."

"Okay, okay, so you've told me."

I did not want to hear any more. Sea Change scared me, and suddenly I found myself caring more about this whole business than seemed reasonable. I wanted Joie de Vivre to win today, but I wanted much more for him to win the Flamingo, and the classic races beyond. I wanted him to win the Derby, just as Chateaugay had done. Now Barnaby Blaine, the expert, starts telling me about a horse who might be better. For reassurance, I went to the paddock to watch Joie de Vivre get saddled for his race.

He looked handsomer than ever. Tall as I'd remembered him, though he seemed to have grown heavier over the winter. I noticed that he was not as big as Sea Change but in no other way did he look any less of a champion. His chestnut coat glistened in late-afternoon sun. He stood calmly, self-assured, as the cinches were tightened around his midsection and the racing bit inserted in his mouth. I was standing right up against the rope, less than ten feet from his stall. He turned his head slightly and his right eye was pointed at me. I felt like waving and saying hello. "Hey! Hi! Remember me? I bet five hundred dollars on you at Belmont."

He walked easily to the walking ring, not a bandage in sight. Rand, the jockey, wearing silks of yellow and white, entered the walking ring and shook hands with the owner and trainer. He was grinning as he looked sideways at the horse. When the time came to mount, Rand patted the horse on the shoulders, then put a foot in the stirrup and climbed aboard.

As Joie de Vivre walked slowly toward the track, I found myself thinking that he would be making that same walk in three months at Churchill Downs. While the band played "My Old Kentucky Home." Goddamnit, I decided, I would be there.

That was when I almost made a bet. In fact, I almost bet $500. The odds board showed Joie de Vivre, surprisingly, at 6–5. That, apparently, was because he had not yet raced this year and because there was a speedy California horse named Cousin George in the race.

All right, I decided. Five hundred dollars to win. Just then I felt a hand on my elbow. It was Jennifer. She was smiling and looking so lovely, with late-afternoon sunshine all around her, that I suddenly wanted to kiss her.

So I did. Right there at the edge of the walking ring. As people stared.

She blushed. It was the first time I had seen her blush. I do not think she considered blushing part of her image.

"I'm happy," she said softly.

"So am I."

The crowd moved past us, toward the windows.

"Hey," I said. "I've got to bet."

"Oh, no. No, you can't. That's what Barnaby was afraid of. That's why he sent me down here. To make sure you wouldn't bet."

"But I love this horse. I love this horse more than I love people."

"Barnaby just told me that emotional attachments to a horse are far more insidious and destructive than emotional attachments to a woman."

"That's easy for him to say. He's never been in love with a horse."

"He says it's like the drama critic having an affair with the leading lady."

"Joie de Vivre will win by eight lengths."

"Barnaby said if you bet this race, he wasn't going to tell you anything else all week."

"But, Jennifer—"

"Let's go back and sit down. If you love the horse, you can be happy if he wins even if you haven't made a bet."

"Yeah, sure I can be happy. But why not be happy and make six hundred dollars besides?"

"Barnaby doesn't approve." She took my hand and started walking. I followed, feeling guilty that this woman had made me unfaithful to my horse.

For some reason, Joie de Vivre was slow leaving the gate. I had been watching carefully through my binoculars and he had seemed to be standing straight, balanced, and poised. But when the starter pushed the button that sprang the doors open electronically, he was last to jump forward. Not left terribly far behind, just not up front where I had hoped he would be. Cousin George was up front. All by himself, three lengths ahead, as he sprinted down the backstretch.

Six-furlong races at Hialeah start near the top of the backstretch, which means there is more than a quarter-mile to be run before the horses reach the turn. This worked to Joie de Vivre's advantage, because it gave him time to move forward before Rand had to worry about establishing good position on the turn. By the time Cousin George had reached the start of the turn, four lengths ahead, Joie de Vivre had passed all the other horses and had enough open space behind him so Rand could move him close to the rail to save ground.

They went around the turn that way, Cousin George sprinting as fast as he could, four lengths ahead. Rand, still not asking Joie de Vivre for anything, measuring his distances—between himself and the leader, and between the leader and the finish line—in second place.

Toward the end of the turn, there is a pole along the rail, a red-and-white-striped pole, that indicates to the jockeys that there is a quarter-mile to go before the finish. When Joie de Vivre reached this pole, with Cousin George already straightening out in the stretch, Rand leaned forward and applied pressure to the horse's neck with his hands, urging him to move faster.

From half a mile away in the clubhouse, I could clearly see the result. Joie de Vivre seemed to jump forward with suddenly longer, harder strides. Cousin George, tiring now, had his lead cut back to three lengths, and as they reached the three-sixteenths pole, to two.

They came through the stretch that way, Cousin George losing ground with every stride. With an eighth of a mile to go, the lead was down to one length; at the sixteenth pole, they were even. By the finish, without further urging from Rand, Joie de Vivre was a length and a half ahead and drawing away. Cousin George was second and no one else was close.

"Barnaby, Barnaby, he is a great horse!"

"What's so great? He catches cheap speed."

"Bullshit. Look at the way he did it. Look at—"

"All right, all right." Blaine was laughing. He held up a hand. "I'm only kidding. He looks like a hell of a horse. In fact, look at that time."

The figures were posted on the board. Joie de Vivre had run the six furlongs in one minute, nine and one-fifth seconds, which was only two-fifths of a second above the track record for the distance. And this had been the first start of his three-year-old year.

"Yeah," Blaine said. "You might be right. He might be a hell of a horse."

The funny thing about the rest of the afternoon was that the two other horses we bet on both lost. And one of them, because he went off at a price of 9–2, we bet twice: to win and to place. When you bet to place, you collect if your horse finishes either first or second, although, naturally, you do not collect as much as you do on a win bet. Blaine said he bet to place only when a horse went off at odds of 4–1 or higher, because only at that price or better, he said, did the potential return justify the risk.

## The Dream Team

I wound up losing $400 for the afternoon, which made it the most money I'd ever lost at a race track in one day, but I was not bothered in the least. Anybody can lose three races in a row, even an expert like Blaine. I still had plenty of money left. With one win the next day, at any kind of a price, I would be even.

Besides, I was exhilarated about Joie de Vivre. And delighted with Jennifer. It looked like it was going to be a great week. The kind of week that I would not want to end. The one consolation would be that Saturday, the last day of the week, was also the day when Joie de Vivre would meet Sea Change in the Flamingo.

We ate dinner in the hotel again. Blaine said he was too tired to go out. I did not want to go out. All there was out was Miami Beach. I did not want to go to Miami Beach. I wanted to go back to Hialeah. And win.

"I hope you're not going to get bored with all this," Blaine said to Jennifer during the meal.

"Are you kidding?" she said. "This is the most exciting week of my life."

"Yes, but six straight days at the race track."

"But we're there with you. With an expert. And that's exciting. I'm terribly stimulated by expertise, no matter what the field." She reached across the table and squeezed his hand. "I could watch a cobbler for a week in San Francisco, doing nothing but making shoes every day. And if I knew he was the *best* cobbler in San Francisco, I'd be excited. That's how I feel about you."

Not long afterward I took her up to bed. Both of us

were tired. We made love in friendly fashion, with the lights on. Then we did it again, for some reason more frenzied the second time. We lay together, the lights still on, my back stinging where the sweat had dripped into the scratches Jennifer had made. She rubbed her hands across the sweat.

"Two sweaty snakes," she said. She reached up and turned off the light. Then she lay down, close to me again. "Two sweaty snakes in the dark."

# Tuesday

"WHAT DO YOU think of me?"

"Huh?"

"I'm starting to worry. I'm afraid you're not taking me seriously."

"What?" I had been sleeping soundly, dreaming of a basketball game in which I was making thirty-foot jump shots and driving the crowd into a frenzy. Now I was awake, with Jennifer sitting over me again.

"I was just thinking about the way I've been acting. Especially Sunday night. You must have thought I was a pretty silly girl."

I propped myself up on one elbow. The room was gray instead of yellow. I looked outside and saw rain. Jennifer was sitting cross-legged on my bed. Wearing a pale blue nightgown and curling loops of her hair around her index fingers.

"It's a wonder you didn't pack me right back to San Francisco. It's a wonder you gave me time to adjust. The fact that you did must mean you care about me."

"What time is it?"

"It's just that I was so scared. You'll have to try to understand that. I lost complete control on Sunday night, and I very seldom do that any more."

I sat up. "Is there any ginger ale in the refrigerator?"

"I didn't say anything I didn't mean. But I realize now that some of what I said was out of place at the time I said it. Do you understand?"

"Ice water, even. Just a tall glass of water with ice."

"Like caring so much about you being famous. Gosh, that's nothing to come right out and say the very first day I'm with you. Especially before we've even been to bed. And the funny thing is I should know better. In my self-control program I've been working very hard on impulses like that."

I got out of bed and went to the bathroom and ran cold water from the tap.

"What I feel for you is very special," she called after me, "and to talk about such a feeling when it's in its very early stages, like it was on Sunday, is to risk destroying it. Don't you think so? I mean, it's like a fetus. It has to be nurtured privately for a while. Until it's ready to withstand the light of day."

94

I stepped back into the bedroom. The rain was falling steadily. "Sloppy track," I said.

She looked at me standing slack-bellied before her. "What?"

I pointed at the window and the rain. "Going to be a sloppy track this afternoon."

She got up and knelt on the mattress. Reaching out, she put her arms around me and pulled me toward her. She held me tightly and put her head against my chest. "I have such enormous potential as a human being," she said. "It would be criminal to waste an ounce. Do you understand that?"

"Sure, Jennifer. Sure."

"I hope so. That's why I have to be very careful of who I let myself get close to. I can only allow myself to feel things for a person who wants what's best for me."

"I think that's a very intelligent attitude."

"It's not an attitude. It's a way of life." She stepped off the mattress and stood in front of me, staring intently into my eyes. "What do you think I'm capable of? How much do you think I can achieve?"

"I don't know what you mean. In what areas?"

"In *life*."

I shrugged. "I don't know. Quite a bit, I guess."

"Do you think I can win a Pulitzer Prize?"

"I don't know. I've never read anything you've written."

"But you know me."

"Yes."

"So? Do you think I can win a Pulitzer Prize? Do you think I'm of that caliber as a person?"

"Sure."

"So you think I can win the prize."

"I guess so. If you get lucky."

"Wrong. That's the wrong answer. I don't believe in luck."

"Well, that's one thing you and Barnaby have in common."

"I don't mean at the horse races. I'm talking about achieving the goals of my life. I've got all the natural attributes. I'm pretty, I'm smart. I know that. I'm not being egotistical; I'm only making a realistic assessment of my strengths. And most important, I'm determined."

"What about your weaknesses?" I said.

"God, you're perceptive. You've put your finger right into the core of this conversation. That's what I've been trying to lead up to. My weaknesses are hard to figure out. At least for me. I look in the mirror, I look into my soul and what I see is so good that it scares me. I know I must be flawed. I don't mean by drinking too much, or talking too much, or caring too much about myself. I mean in some serious way. But how? I don't know. And I've been making an honest self-examination, trying to find out."

"Well—"

"You can help me. We're living together for a week. Already we've shared intimate knowledge of each other. I intend to continue to bare myself to you—not just physically, but in conversations like this. At the end of the week, you'll know me almost as well as I know myself. And from the special vantage point that you'll have, and with the kind of insight you've got, I know you can tell me some terribly important things about myself."

"Jennifer—"

"Do you know what I want you to do? At the end of the week? On our last night here? After we've made love for the last time I want you to go into the living room and sit at the table and write out an assessment of me. Not as a sex object but as a person. Show me no mercy. Put down every flaw. You can give it to me in a sealed envelope Sunday morning and I can read it after I've gotten on the plane. That way you won't have to worry about embarrassing me."

"Jennifer, I really don't think—"

"I promise I'll be completely open and honest with you at all times. I'll relax and be completely myself. No more trying to make an impression."

"I hadn't realized you were."

She pinched my cheek. "Silly. You weren't supposed to. But come on. Promise me. It would prove to me you really care."

"I'm sorry, Jennifer. But I don't make promises before breakfast."

She stripped off her nightgown and started to do calisthenics. "See," she said, breathing hard, doing sit-ups. "Ordinarily I'd do these somewhere where you couldn't see me." She went down again and came up. "But now that I'm being myself . . . I can . . . let it all . . . hang out."

Later, while we were taking our shower together, Jennifer said, "Listen, if you want to take notes, that's perfectly all right. Because I'll be taking notes about you."

"What?"

97

"It's just an impression I'm forming, but I'm starting to think that it's been quite some time since anyone has given you an honest assessment of what you are."

Immediately after our shower, we made love. Jennifer was relentless, driving her body like a piston. I could not decide whether she was fueled by desire or whether it was just another aspect of her determination to excel.

The leading jockey at Hialeah that year was a nineteen-year-old apprentice named Sonny Holiday. He had ridden twenty-two winners for the meeting. The jockey closest to him had twelve.

It seemed to be that way at Hialeah every year; in fact, it was that way at the big tracks everywhere. A new kid every year. Each supposed to be the greatest since Arcaro. You would come back the next year, and they'd be gone.

Holiday, like all the others, was supposed to be different. He was supposed to be one who would last.

"He's got one thing going for him," Blaine said. "He's not a Latin. That can make him very popular around Miami."

It was true. For the past few years the hot apprentices had come from Panama or Puerto Rico or Venezuela. But Holiday, who had strawberry-blond hair, had been born and raised in South Dakota. Finally: an American. A hero for whom the Kiwanis Club of Coral Gables could really root when its members enjoyed their annual outing at the track.

An apprentice jockey is one who is just starting to ride. To make up for his inexperience, the horses he rides are allowed to carry less weight. This advantage starts at ten pounds and works down to five as the rider starts to win: the weight being made up of the jockey's own weight plus lead weights carried in the saddle bags. It seems strange, but even on a half-ton horse, five pounds can make a difference.

Apprentices are particularly useful on fast horses in short races, where judgment and skill are not as important as the break in the weights. All the rider has to do is make sure he doesn't fall off; for six furlongs, a fast horse can do the rest.

Jockeys who ride fast horses in short races tend to win a lot. So there usually is an apprentice or two among the leading jockeys at any major track. It is a quick road to glory, but unfortunately, it doesn't end there.

One day, a year from the date he rode his first winner (or after he has ridden his hundredth, if that should happen to come first), the apprentice's weight allowance is taken away. He now has to compete with the regular jockeys on even terms. The same trainer who three weeks ago was pleading with him to ride is suddenly too busy to talk. And all of his horses have riders. Riders like Shoemaker or Baeza or Cordero or Pincay. At the same weights, why should the trainer use the kid? He wants the best for his horse; and if it is a break in the weights he is looking for, then there's always the new hot apprentice.

So the kid shoots a lot of pool in the jockeys' room in the afternoons, and maybe starts working out horses in the morning—and listens silently as the big names, or the new hot apprentice, come back laughing about how easy it was to win with the horse the kid rode last month.

Maybe he gets a couple of 20– or 30–1 shots. They finish where 20– and 30–1 shots are supposed to. After a couple of months of this, there's suddenly no money for the payment on the Cadillac, or for $150 outfits for the girl friend who taught him so much about bed.

So the kid takes off. To New England or Canada or the midwest. Wherever there are horses to ride. Cheap horses. The kind that couldn't make it in the big time. Generally, the Cadillac and the girl friend stay behind.

Sometimes these apprentices come back. Occasionally, like with Bobby Woodhouse in New York, they are good enough so they never have to go away. The trouble is they never know until it happens. All they know the first year is that they're winning, and at nineteen it is hard to imagine that winning ever could stop.

There was a story about Sonny Holiday in the *Miami Herald* Tuesday morning. He had ridden three winners the day before. This made Jennifer excited. He was the best jockey on the grounds and she wanted to know more about him. Barnaby explained that he wasn't the best— only the winningest—but that made him all the more appealing. We went to the walking ring to look at him before the second race. The rain had stopped. We had no bet until the fourth.

He was the first jockey into the ring, walking alone, his eyes already on his horse. There were a few shouts of "Hey, Sonny" from people leaning against the fence getting their feet wet. Holiday paid no attention. He was wearing white silks with royal-blue stripes. He stood erect beneath a tree as he received instructions from his trainer. Even as the trainer spoke, Holiday did not look at his face. He looked instead at the palm trees and the sky. He was small, even for a jockey, able to make weight of 108 pounds, including silks and boots. His face was pale and blank, with small, pinched features. He seemed to have absorbed the personality of the little town in South Dakota that he came from. The story in the *Herald* had said that he'd run away four years before, at the age of fifteen, because he had not liked school and he was too small to make a living farming wheat. He seemed to carry the barren winter and the remoteness with him yet. The trainer spoke of strategy; Holiday seemed to hear instead train whistles in the night and the sweep of wind across empty plains.

He mounted his horse without acknowledging the assistance of the trainer. Twice the field walked the grassy circle before going to the track. Holiday sat straight and still on his horse's back, wrapping the reins around his left hand and tying a knot in them with his right. Some of the other jockeys smiled at the crowd or made remarks to friends along the fence, or talked to the rider of the stable pony that walked beside them. Holiday spoke to no one. He stared straight ahead, with no expression on his face.

What struck me most about him were his eyes. The eyes belonged in a firing squad. I could see them staring down the barrel, just as they stared now at the trees. Unblinking even when the trigger was pulled.

He looked younger than nineteen, but to call him boyish would be accurate only if one meant the kind of boy who could burn a fly's wings off or stone a frog to death without emotion. By the time the horses left the walking ring, I had goosebumps on my neck and wasn't sure why.

"A cold one, that kid."

"Huh?"

"Holiday. He's a cold one," a man standing next to me said.

I nodded.

"And hungry," the man said. "That one don't want to go home."

The race was at one mile and an eighth, for horses who could be claimed for $9,000. For once, Holiday was on a weak horse, going off at 15–1.

He broke in the middle of the twelve-horse field but trailed the leaders badly through the first half-mile. The track was still soft from the rains, and Holiday's horse did not seem to like it. He passed a couple of horses toward the end of the backstretch, but more because they came back to him than because he went after them. The leaders were still ten lengths ahead. I watched carefully through my binoculars, but a mist made the final turn hard to see. Holiday was wearing a white cap, and although the rest of him was covered with mud, somehow the cap had stayed clean. I saw him flip down another pair of goggles —on muddy or sloppy tracks, riders will wear four or five pair, and flip the top one off as soon as it gets dirty—and hold his horse close to the rail on the turn. Toward the end of the turn I saw him go to his whip. Three, four times he hit his horse, and the cheap and tired thing began to run. But there seemed to be nowhere to go. There were two tiers of horses ahead: two lengths in front of him were three horses running side by side; five lengths further up, almost certainly out of reach, were two more fighting for the lead.

The obvious move for Holiday was to swing wide around the turn, get a clear track ahead of him, and let his horse run through the stretch. If his horse had any kind of strength left, he might pass the second tier and gain third place, which was more than could be expected at 15–1.

But Holiday did not make the obvious move. He ran right up on the heels of the second tier on the turn. As they came off it, and straightened for the homestretch, centrifugal force pulled each of them a bit to the outside. Suddenly there was room—not much; just a flash of day-light—along the inside rail. Rather than circle, Holiday leaned left and thrust his horse toward this gap. It meant driving a 1,000-pound animal forty miles an hour through a three-and-a-half-foot alley that might close at any mo-ment—something like driving through a tollgate with the gas pedal on the floor and the booths moving back and forth across the road. It was a cheap race, he had a horse that no one expected much from, there was the unyielding wooden rail on one side and the swaying hindquarters of a horse on the other; the track beneath was slippery with rain and mud—but Holiday never hesitated. He whipped his horse twice more, almost grazing the shoulders of the jockey to his right, and burst through the gap.

He had saved at least five lengths by taking the risk. He not only swept by the second tier, but he caught one of the two leaders at the finish. The other, the 8–5 favorite, held on to win by a neck.

So Holiday's daring had made the difference between second and third places in a race that was forgotten by all concerned the minute it was over. For Holiday, who got ten percent of his horse's share of the purse, in addition to a $50 riding fee, the difference was less than $100.

"He's not the only jockey in the country who would have done that in a cheap race," Blaine said. "But I couldn't name you half a dozen."

I watched as he brought his horse back to be unsaddled. The groom who came to meet him was smiling and seemed about to kiss the horse. Probably he had bet to place or show.

Holiday dismounted without a word. The groom seemed to be talking to him, but Holiday turned his back. Before walking to the scales to weigh in, Holiday turned to the horse and hit him hard on the side of the neck. It did not seem a gesture of affection.

When Holiday turned again and I saw his face, I knew the reason for the slap. It had been an outlet for frustration. Holiday was angry that he had not won the race.

I did not know how much Blaine was betting. He did not volunteer the information and it was the sort of question one did not ask. He came with me to the $100 window, but betting at the $100 window is like going to confession: a very private matter. There was a wooden partition built outside and an armed guard standing alongside, and the bettors filed in one by one so no one would know what anyone else was doing. Blaine could have been betting $100, as I was, or he could have been betting $1,000.

The people at the $100 window did not look any smarter than the people anywhere else at the track. Just slightly better dressed; more expensively dressed anyway, not necessarily dressed with better taste. Back in the days when I thought people who bet big money were smart, I spent fifteen minutes hanging around the $50 window at Aqueduct to see who the insiders liked. The first eight people to the window each bet a different horse. They all lost. The only thing Blaine had told me about betting was that it was wiser to bet a certain percentage of your capital on each race, rather than to bet a flat amount. He suggested five percent, which, as it worked out, was exactly what I had done on Monday. But after losing $400, my capital was only $1,600, so five percent would mean $80 bets. That was the principle behind the theory: cut back when you're losing and bet bigger when you win.

I decided not to do it. We would start winning soon enough, and I didn't want to be stuck making smaller bets when we did. I would stay at $100 until we won, and then, when my total climbed above $2,000, I would start to bet five percent.

There were only two horses to bet all afternoon. A 6–5 favorite in the fourth race and a horse that went off at 6–1 in the ninth. We bet that one win and place because of the higher price.

Both finished out of the money. Which left me $300

behind for the day and $700 down for the trip. A slow start, Blaine said. But it had happened frequently in the past.

The good news of the day was about Joie de Vivre. The *Morning Telegraph* story said he had come out of Monday's race in perfect condition, with no sign of the ankle trouble from last year. He definitely would start in the Flamingo. Then there were a couple of quotes from Rand about how the race had been much easier than it probably had looked from the stands. "I only asked him for speed," Rand said. "I didn't demand it. And I only asked him once." Then Rand had been asked about the Flamingo. If he thought Joie de Vivre could run a mile and an eighth. And how he thought he'd do against Sea Change. "I never rode the other horse, so I can't say anything about that. But my horse feels like he wants to run all day. He feels like a champion and I'm happy to be his rider."

That was the kind of talk I liked to hear. "Feels like a champion." And Rand was not a big-mouth. If he said that about a horse, it meant something. On the same page there was a story about Sea Change. His owner said flatly that he expected to win the Flamingo and all the races beyond. "The longer they get," he said, "the better we like it." He talked as if he actually ran the distances alongside the horse. Regarding Joie de Vivre, he said he saw little to compare. "That other is a pretty nice race horse, but in Sea Change I believe we own an immortal."

We left after the ninth race as rain started falling again. The crowd was betting Holiday as if he were Jesus.

Horses of his that should have been 4–1 were 5–2 because he was the rider. It was the way New York used to be with Arcaro. They would bet a mediocre horse down to favorite because Arcaro was the jockey, and then, when the horse would lose as he deserved to, they would charge the rail and boo Arcaro because he had lost again on a favorite.

The only difference was that Holiday was not losing. He had three winners for the second day in a row.

"Gosh," Jennifer said in the car, "we should forget all your figuring, Barnaby, and just bet on Holiday's horses."

He glared at her.

"Just think how much we would have made these past two days if we'd done that."

"How about some music, sweetheart. On the radio."

"Six winners in two days? And we haven't had one."

"Turn it up, please," Blaine said. "I like this song." It was Simon and Garfunkel: "Bridge Over Troubled Waters."

"Maybe tomorrow we should just bet the horses Holiday rides."

Then I pinched her knee and she was quiet. Blaine tapped the steering wheel and whistled as he drove.

We drank a lot at dinner. Jennifer said rain depressed her and made her want to drink. Blaine said it made him want to lie in his bed and read mystery stories. As soon as dinner was over, he left us in order to do that. I was hoping we would win the next day. We had decided, kind of as a joke on Monday morning, that we would eat in the hotel on nights we lost—because I could put it on my expense account—and go out to dinner when we won.

Three straight nights in the hotel now, and the joke was not quite so funny. Jennifer drank three martinis before dinner, even though she said all she normally drank was Scotch. We had two bottles of wine with the meal, and Jennifer drank at least one and a half. I was hoping that this would not be another Sunday night.

When Blaine left us I asked Jennifer what she wanted to do.

"Go up to the room," she said. "And play my game."

"What's your game?"

She leaned close to me and whispered, "I'll show you when we get there." She was wearing a tan cashmere sweater and brown leather skirt. She said she did not like leather but she wore it because she knew it was arousing.

The lobby of the hotel was empty even though it was only nine o'clock at night. Jennifer suddenly started to sing and clap her hands and dance as we waited for the elevator.

"I can't get no—sat-is-fact-shun." She broke off. "God, I wish we had a phonograph. Just think, we could have music every night."

"Wait until we win," I said. "I'll buy you one."

"If you really had style, you'd do it anyway."

"What? Fifty bucks for a phonograph that we leave behind when we go?"

"Why not? You're rich. Why not live a little, and show me a good time?"

We got to the room. Jennifer kicked off her shoes, spun around and faced me, in the middle of the living room, her hands on her hips.

"What's your game?" I said.

"Sex fantasies."

"What?"

"We act out roles. And we have sexual confrontations in our roles."

"I don't think I understand you."

"It's really a turn-on. Oh God, I only wish we had some grass. When you're stoned, it gets freaky. Anyway, here's how we do it. I play a role, and then you play whatever role is the most erotically arousing to go with it. For instance: I'm the high school cheerleader. I'm a senior and I'm the most beautiful and the sexiest girl in the school. Not only have I dated five or six guys from the football team all at once, but I even go away some weekends to date guys who are big names in college. Now, suddenly, I'm at a party. And you're at the party, too. Only you're just a skinny little sophomore with acne on his face. You've only just started to masturbate and you've never, never even made out with a girl. You're shy, but you're the scholarly type, and I get into a conversation with you because I like intelligent conversation. Only the whole thing is too much for you. You don't know whether you're going to shoot a load in your pants or run away. And then I start getting friendly. I say, very demurely, 'I wouldn't mind if you asked me to dance.' The lights are low. *And* it's an unchaperoned party. With empty bedrooms upstairs. Okay, we can pick it up from there."

"Jennifer, Jesus Christ. That's the most ridiculous thing I've ever heard of in my life."

"What's wrong?"

"It's stupid, that's what's wrong. It doesn't make any sense."

"Oh, I know what the trouble is. You're too worried about your masculinity to be willing to accept an inferior role. Okay, how about this one. You're the brilliant young assistant managing editor of *Time* magazine. First in your class at Yale, a brilliant yachtsman and tennis player and the obvious heir apparent. You've also got one of the biggest harems in New York. There's nobody you want you haven't slept with. You've got Gloria Steinem eating out of your hand.

"I'm in my first week on the staff as a researcher. I only graduated from Smith two months before. I'm beautiful and sexually I'm very with it. But I just haven't met any guys in New York who've turned me on. I'm so low on the corporate totem pole I normally wouldn't even be allowed to see you, but there's a crash project for the next week's issue and everybody is working late and two other girls in my department are out sick. So at eight o'clock on Friday night I suddenly turn up at your office. You've never seen me before. I've heard of you, of course; all New York has heard of you. And once I've even ridden with you in an elevator. My knees are shaking because for the first time you're going to speak to me. I've got some important material relating to the project. I walk into your office and you look up from your desk and say, 'Yes, what is it?' in a very snappish tone. Out of the corner of my eye I can't help but notice the long black leather couch beneath the futuristic sculpture next to your desk."

"Wait a minute, wait a minute. That's enough."

She was smiling. "I know. I was finished. This is where we start. Why don't you pull a chair up to the end of the coffee table. We can pretend that's your desk. But it's better if you put a necktie on. Wouldn't you be wearing a necktie in your office?"

"Jennifer, stop! I'm not going to play."

The smile vanished. "What do you mean?"

"I mean I'm not going to play these games. They're absurd."

"They'll add spice to our relationship. We can't let ourselves be bound by inhibitions."

"Who's inhibited?"

"You are. Because you won't play my games."

"That's ridiculous."

"You're constricted."

"And you're nuts. Now come here. You and I are going to bed together. No high school cheerleaders or—Jesus Christ, what's so erotic about that anyway?—*Time* magazine editors are going to get in the way."

"No! You and I are not going to bed together. Not after you've made that kind of fool out of me. And—by the way—*Time* magazine editors happen to have power. And power just happens to be erotic."

She walked into the bedroom and slammed the door behind her. Then I heard her pushing furniture around. I tried the door but it was blocked.

"You sleep out there tonight!" she yelled through the door. "And maybe tomorrow you won't be afraid to live!"

"Jennifer, if you don't open that door within sixty seconds I am going to pick up the telephone and tell the front desk that there is a drunken woman in my room, and you'll be eating breakfast in San Francisco tomorrow morning."

She moved the furniture away from the door. But she remained very unhappy. "That wasn't playing fair," she said. "You were supposed to threaten to break down the door and then beat me senseless if I didn't let you in."

"I wouldn't do that, Jennifer. I've never hit a woman in my life."

"You ought to try it sometime. It might break down some inhibitions."

She would not make love to me that night. She kissed me good night like a sister, put on her nightgown in the closet, and climbed into the bed by the window.

"Good night," she said, and rolled on her side away from me.

I got under the covers and turned out the light. For what must have been twenty minutes, neither of us spoke.

Then Jennifer said, "You hurt me very badly."

"I'm sorry. But you were being ridiculous."

"I was doing it for your own good."

"What?"

"I don't want to be one woman to you. I want to be many women."

"I'm afraid I don't understand you again."

"Men get tired of one woman, no matter how much they give. I don't want you ever to get tired of me."

"Jennifer, I'm not likely to get tired of you in the next four days."

"I'm thinking beyond that. And it's happened in my

very own home. My father has started to sleep with other women. Despite the fact that my mother is the most sexual woman I've ever seen."

"How do you know?"

"I've listened to her in bed. My room used to be next to theirs. I'd get out of bed and listen at the wall."

"I mean, how do you know your father is sleeping with other women?"

"I've seen him. Not actually in bed. But I've followed him around the city, when he does a morning operation and leaves the hospital in early afternoon. I've seen him eating lunch with three different women. And every time they've gone together into a hotel."

"Did you ever talk to him about it?"

"Why should I? It's his life. All it did was teach me a lesson. That kind of thing is never going to happen to me. I thought for a long time and finally figured out why it happened to my mother. No matter how sexual she was, she was just my mother. His wife. And he got bored with that after twenty years. No man is ever going to get bored with me. Not even if I have to drag him kicking and screaming into areas of eroticism that he's afraid of."

"Jennifer, I wasn't afraid of that. It just seemed ridiculous."

"That's because you *are* afraid. It's a deep-seated block. And I bet I know where it came from."

She sat up in bed now. I could see her silhouette, dark against the gray sky beyond the window.

"You went to Catholic schools."

"Huh?"

"Didn't you go to Catholic schools?"

"Yeah, but so what?"

"I knew it. That's why you're constricted." She lay down again in the bed. "Don't worry. It's something we can work out together over a period of time."

"Jennifer, we've only got four more days. I hate to keep reminding you, but this is for only one week."

"But I'm already thinking up excuses for you to come to Salt Lake City. We can ski there even in April. Somebody told me Robert Redford owns a ski lodge. Maybe we can go skiing with Robert Redford. And do you know what I'll do between now and the time you come? Charcoal sketches. I'll sketch us in various positions of making love. And then when you come, we can duplicate some of the things that I've drawn. I think that would be a good way to start working on your constrictions."

She sat up again in her bed. Then she climbed out of it and came to mine. "Do you know what we had tonight?"

"What?"

"Our first quarrel."

"Oh."

"Isn't that romantic? And we've emerged from it even closer than before. That's such a good sign." She squeezed my shoulders with her hands and kissed me on the cheek. Then she climbed back into her bed and lay down. She was silent for another ten minutes and I thought she was sleeping, but then she spoke, softly, facing the window, where a moon was starting to shine through the clouds. "Do you know what this is?" she said.

"No, Jennifer. I don't know what this is."

"It's the honeymoon."

"The what?"

"The honeymoon. With the courtship and marriage still to follow." Then she giggled a couple of times and fell silent.

A few minutes later she was asleep. I could tell by the regular, heavy breathing. Soon she began to snore. Not loudly, but enough to keep me awake. She would sleep uninterrupted until morning. That was why she insisted on sleeping in her own bed, she had told me. The importance of uninterrupted sleep. She was convinced that the reason most people began to show their age in their fifties and got frail in their sixties was because through almost all their adult lives their sleep had been interrupted. This was nothing that anyone had ever told her. Just something she had figured out for herself.

# Wednesday

WE ATE BREAKFAST with Blaine in his suite. The waiter wheeled the table in through a path that Blaine had cleared among his *Morning Telegraphs* on the floor. Jennifer did not eat, of course, but she drank four glasses of fresh orange juice at $2.25 apiece, tax not included. She also ordered a bottle of mineral water for $3, which meant she had spent $12, plus tax, for breakfast, without having put a morsel of food into her mouth.

"Tap water in strange cities," she said, smiling, "simply *devastates* my bowels."

Outside, the sky was the color of slush. Rain was fall-

ing. Blaine said it had been drizzling at least since five
A.M. when he had walked downtown for the *Telegraphs*.
He now had, next to all his other equipment on the bar, a
thick binder with a hard cover on which the words *Rain
Manual* had been stenciled. It contained computations,
which he had made himself over twenty-five years, of
what each tenth of an inch of rain over a twenty-four-
hour span did to the speed of the race track. He had
separate computations for thirty-two race tracks in North
America that he either had visited or planned to. The
weather information required to keep these computations
up to date cost him more than a thousand dollars a year to
obtain. Then, different equations had to be made for
different months of the year, because, as he said, "November rain at Aqueduct is very different from July rain."

Blaine had not been to Aqueduct since 1961, but if he
ever went again, in the rain, he would be ready. At home,
he also had wind charts for Santa Anita and Hollywood
Park, showing the direction and mean strength of the
prevailing winds at different key points around the course.

Jennifer wrote it all down in her notebook. "Will the
rain affect your betting today?" she asked.

"I've spoken to the weather bureau twice already. They
predict rain all day, so I've made my estimates based on
that. If it stops, I may have to revise, but that's no problem, I'll just bring the Rain Manual to the track."

"How about if it keeps raining?"

"Then we're in fine shape. Our horse has a very good
chance."

"Our horse?" I said.

"Right. We've got a bet in the eighth race today."

"And nothing before?"

Blaine shook his head.

"But that's ridiculous," Jennifer said.

"Sorry, sweetheart. I don't put the races together, I only try to pick them apart."

"But you've come all this way for one week of betting horses and now you're only betting once all day?"

"That's right. Christ, there's nothing so unusual about it. A couple of years ago at Saratoga I didn't make a bet for four days."

"But then it's a waste of time," Jennifer said.

"It's a bigger waste to bet stupidly for four days and lose."

"But at least it's exciting."

"There's nothing exciting about losing."

"But what are you going to do all day?"

"Well, I'll tell you. There's some work I want to do with my pace cards."

"Sorry," Jennifer said. "I don't understand."

"My index cards. That I use to evaluate early speed as opposed to late speed. After the first race we'll have been here long enough for me to run a twenty-one-race check and establish some meaningful variables for the second half of the week."

Jennifer closed her notebook and put it away. "Barnaby? Can I borrow your car today? I want to go to Key West."

It turned out that Jennifer wanted to go to Key West because she had read about it in a book by Ernest Hemingway and she thought it would be romantic. She thought it would be romantic to go anywhere she had read about in books by Ernest Hemingway. France, Italy, Spain, Africa: once she made The Dream Team, she would get to see them all. Meanwhile, Key West might help her make The Dream Team. She had an idea for a story. Another story, to go with the one on Blaine.

"I've already got it outlined in my mind. A mood piece. Key West on a rainy winter afternoon. The ghost of Hemingway brooding over the town."

"Jennifer," I said. "It's a hundred and twenty miles."

"So? That's only a two-hour ride."

"Not in my car," Blaine said. "Not at twelve cents a mile. Besides, we need the car for the track."

"You can take a cab to the track," Jennifer said. "Please? This could be a very important opportunity for me."

"Come on, Jennifer," I said. "Be serious."

"I am serious. I think it's a much more serious idea to go to Key West and write something about one of our native American geniuses than to go to a silly old race track *and then not even make a bet!*"

"We are making a bet," Blaine said. "One bet. Besides, Hemingway was a fraud."

"What do you *mean?*"

"Posturing. All his work is posturing."

"It's *genius!*" Jennifer shouted. "His works are works of genius."

"Narrow posturing at that. All he knew was bullfighting and war."

"But they're metaphors for existence!"

119

Blaine winked at me and chuckled. "We're going to the races in ten minutes," he said. "In my car. Anyone who wants to come is welcome."

I took Jennifer by the hand and walked her toward the door.

"You're jealous of his masculinity!" she shouted at Blaine. He chuckled again. At the door she paused and turned. I was already out in the hall. "I bet when Ernest Hemingway went to the horse races he made more than one bet a day!" she said.

She slammed the door behind her as she left.

We had a brief argument in the room. She wanted me to go downstairs and rent a car for her to drive to Key West. When I refused she called me cheap and said I didn't care about her career. Then she apologized. She said she usually didn't behave that way but she was very tense about making The Dream Team. "I've got to do something," she said. "Something that will attract their attention in New York."

"How about a piece on Sonny Holiday?" I meant it as a joke.

"That's it! That's a great idea! That's even better than the story about Barnaby. And think of the impression it will make. 'Who is this girl?' they'll say. 'Who is this girl who can write such a sensitive, stirring portrait about a teen-aged jockey at a race track? If she can do that, she can do anything. I think we need her. I think we'd better bring her to New York!' Yes, yes, that's it. A story on Sonny Holiday. 'Making It Big in a Little Man's World.' 'From Prairie to Post Parade' or 'How're You Going to

Keep Them Down on the Farm When They've Seen the Winner's Circle at Hialeah?' "

She threw her arms around me and kissed me with her greatest enthusiasm of the week. "Thank you," she said. "Thank you so much for that idea."

I didn't tell her it was only a joke. At least, I figured, it would keep her from getting too bored at the track.

Jennifer went directly to the publicity office and explained who she was and what she wanted. They told her it might be difficult to arrange an interview with Holiday, since he was reluctant to talk to reporters, but they could give her plenty of publicity releases about him. No, she said, she wanted an interview. She was sure that once he found out she was a pretty girl reporter, he would not mind. The publicity man at the track told her to check back again in a couple of hours.

Blaine went directly to the veranda bar where he laid his multicolored index cards all over a table. By the time he finished, the table top looked like the grandstand at one of those UCLA football games where the kids spell out Beat the Trojans and make pictures of bears' heads at half-time. I drank soup and shivered in the chilly afternoon. I had no idea what Blaine was doing with his slide rule and Rain Manual, but I hoped it would help.

He worked for four hours. After the first hour I switched from soup to Scotch. Jennifer was gone most of the afternoon, spending it in the publicity office, looking through their files and waiting for an answer from Holiday. She came back once and said the publicity people had suggested she write a story about the flamingos or the tropical gardens instead.

Shortly before the seventh race Blaine gathered up all his cards again. By now my head was buzzing from the Scotch.

"Perfect," he said. "Everything has gone exactly according to form."

I nodded. I wondered if I was supposed to feel reassured.

Then Jennifer came back from the publicity office. I heard her before I saw her. She was calling my name as loud as she could, and racing across the damp gray veranda.

"I got it! I got it! I got the interview!"

"How was he? What did he say?"

"No, not yet, darling. Tonight! I'm meeting him for dinner in Miami Beach."

There were only about a dozen other people in the room, but all of them were staring.

"Hey, calm down. Let's go outside. Tell me all about it."

"He's going to see me. Sonny Holiday. I get to have a whole dinner with him. Oh, what a story this will make. Imagine: the sports pages all over the country."

"But, Jennifer, you haven't even talked to anyone in New York. You have no idea if they even want it."

"They do, they do. I'm sure they do. If you were a newspaper editor, wouldn't you?"

"I don't know. Outside of Florida, hardly anybody has heard of Sonny Holiday."

"All the better. He's fresh copy. And how often do you see a jockey interviewed by a girl?"

She chattered on like that for another twenty minutes. Her dinner appointment was set for seven-thirty at a restaurant called Joe's Stone Crab in the south end of Miami Beach. The publicity people had told her it was one of the best restaurants in Florida. Holiday would meet her there. Barnaby could drop her off on the way back to the hotel. It wouldn't matter if she was early. She could use the time to have a couple of drinks to steady her nerves. After dinner, naturally, Holiday would bring her back to our hotel.

"Okay," I said, "that sounds fine. But you'd better make sure he knows that when he gets you up to your hotel room, it isn't going to be empty."

"Oh, silly. I'm going to tell him all about you. As soon as I'm finished asking him my questions. I'm proud of our relationship. I want everybody to know." Then she giggled and kissed me on the cheek. "Do you know what?"

"What?"

"I called you 'darling' before."

"So I heard."

"And do you know what?"

"What?"

"It sounded pretty nice."

Blaine tapped me on the shoulder. "Let's go to the paddock, lovebird. It's time to look at our horse."

The grassy area behind the clubhouse, where normally bettors studied their form sheets in the sun, was almost

deserted. We walked across the soft earth with our collars
turned up against the drizzle. The air was so humid we
could see our breath when we talked.

The horse for which we had been waiting for four hours
was small and skinny and gray. With bandages on all four
legs. The race it was entered in was six furlongs, with a
$7,500 claiming price for each horse. In each of its past
three races, against the same kind of competition, it had
jumped first from the gate, led by at least five lengths
after half a mile, and held on to win by no less than two.
Still, it had not been claimed. Probably because of its
legs.

"You get the feeling," Blaine said, "that its next stride
might be its last?"

"I sure do."

"Well, I wouldn't buy the son of a bitch for seventy-five
hundred dollars, or even for seventy-five, but I think he's
probably worth a bet."

"Let's go then." He was 7–5 on the board in the early
betting. At that price I would have to bet $500 to get even
for the week. And this horse was no Joie de Vivre. I
thought I would stay at $100 and worry about getting
even tomorrow.

"Let's wait a minute," Blaine said. "Any horse that looks
like this, I want to be sure he can walk."

We stood in the drizzle, staring into the stall. We had
little company on the grass. The trainer came into the
stall, a cigarette hanging from his lips, and began to put
the saddle on the horse. He worked quickly, and it seemed

to me, sloppily, though I knew little about putting saddles on horses.

I noticed that the animal's legs were quivering, and that although the rest of him was speckled gray, his legs were black.

"From standing in ice," Blaine said. "To relieve his soreness."

The horse already was breaking into a white lather, as though the effort of walking from the barn to the paddock had been too much. Then he started to shift uneasily from side to side, as though it hurt him just to stand on legs like those.

The trainer slapped him sharply on the nose and told him to be still, but he kept moving. And now he started to toss his head as if in pain.

"Jesus," Blaine said. "This is pitiful."

We watched for another five minutes, Blaine staring intently at the horse. Then, just as the trainer prepared to lead the horse to the walking ring, he gave one final shift of his hindquarters and squirted a pale brown fluid all over the back of his stall.

"That's it," Blaine said. "No bet. That's a very, very sick horse, and they ought to be ashamed to allow him to race."

We went back to the sidewalk café for a beer instead of making a bet. Jennifer had gone back to the publicity office to pick up pictures of Sonny Holiday to mail to New York with her story.

"It pisses me off," Blaine said, "that a race track like this would even allow that kind of horse on the track."

We watched the race on closed circuit TV from the bar. The horse went off at even money and won by four.

"I don't believe it," Jennifer said. "It really exists."

"What's that?"

"Arthur Godfrey Road. Look." She pointed out the window at the sign. Blaine drove smoothly over the causeway and we were into Miami Beach. Unfortunately for Jennifer, the restaurant was at the unglamorous end of town. Blaine took a right turn and headed south, away from the luxury hotels.

"Oh, darn," Jennifer said. "I wanted to see the Americana. The Fontainebleau."

"Pigstys," Blaine said.

"Expensive pigstys," I added.

I had stayed at the Fontainebleau once. They charged me $60 a day for my room. One night I came in late, after the lobby newsstand was closed. I took a newspaper off the floor of the elevator as I rode up to my room. I left a dime for the paper. "That's twenty cents," the elevator operator said. "No," I said. "It's a dime." He shook his head. "Twenty cents." I said, "But it's a dime at the newsstand." He said, "Yeah, well the newsstand is closed. In the elevator it's twenty cents."

"Miami Beach," Jennifer said. "I can't believe I'm here. It's not New York but it really is part of the American Dream."

Blaine drove past narrow little hotels which had front porches filled with rocking chairs on which old people sat. All the old people looked the same, except some were fat and some were thin. None of them spoke to each other;

none had any expression in his face. They sat on the porches and rocked, or sat on the porches in straight chairs. And stared at the traffic moving past.

"The American Dream, huh?"

"What, Barnaby?"

"I said there's your American Dream, sweetheart. Two hours in a rocking chair after dinner. Watching the traffic go by. And you know what color their rooms are upstairs? Their rooms are the color of their skin."

Jennifer did not want us to wait at the restaurant. She did not want Holiday to see us. She was acting like a girl on a date who does not want her boyfriend to see her father.

"Be home early, dear," I said, and kissed her goodbye.

"I'm so nervous. Almost as nervous as when I met you."

"Relax. If you make a good impression, maybe he'll take you to San Francisco for a week."

She stuck her tongue out at me. "You're just lucky," she said.

"How am I lucky?"

"You're lucky that I love you so much."

I pretended I hadn't heard her. I waved and got back into the car. It was only six-twenty, which gave Jennifer time for two or three drinks.

"Root for me," she called.

"What'd you say?"

"Root for me."

If she had believed in God, she would have said "Pray."

"That, I don't mind telling you, is a load off my mind," Blaine said. We were driving back to the hotel. I had suggested we eat out, but he said no. That would go against his discipline. No restaurants outside the hotel until we had a winning day. So we punished ourselves nightly with $15 wine.

"What's a load off your mind?"

"Getting that broad out of our hair for a few hours."

"You don't like her any more?"

"She's nuts."

"I think she's been behaving pretty well." She had been, at least in public. If Blaine thought she was nutty, I wondered how he would have reacted to her sex games.

"You're going to have to keep her away from me. She's starting to hurt my concentration."

"But you do your work in the mornings. Before she even gets up."

"Yeah, but it's getting to the point where I look at the figures and I see her flirty little smile all over the page. And that voice, I hear that voice in my sleep. She never shuts up. I don't know how you can stand it."

"I have ways of shutting her up."

"I hope they're enjoyable."

"They are. Very."

"I should have let her take my car to Key West. With no money and only enough gas for one way."

"Barnaby. I thought you liked her."

"She's a fruitcake. She probably wouldn't have stopped at Key West. She'd of gone right on down to interview Castro. Or play touch football with Jean-Claude Duvalier."

"I don't know what to say. I'm sorry she's getting on your nerves."

"It's not my nerves. My nerves are fine. It's just at the race track I have to concentrate. I can't keep getting distracted by some broad telling me we should be betting on jockeys. Sonny Holiday, Christ. He'll be lucky if he gets to say ten words during the whole goddamned dinner. Just watch out he doesn't get her too drunk, or you'll never see her again. Remember—she's excited by success."

"I'll see her again."

"That's right. I forgot. Her clothes are in your room. All three tons of them."

"Look, you've got to admit she's well dressed."

"Yeah, she's well dressed. I wonder what style she likes in strait jackets."


At dinner, Blaine drank a lot. More than he had since Sunday afternoon.

"I like having you here, kid."

"I like being here."

"You'd like it more with a couple of winners, huh?"

"They'll come."

"Goddamnit, that's something about you I like. You've got faith. Three days without a winner and you haven't whimpered once."

"Only at night. When you can't hear me."

"I'm starting to think you understand. I'm starting to think you appreciate. You realize what the horses can mean to someone's life."

"Oh, I understand."

"Don't say that glibly. It's not an easy thing. We're talking about obsession, and that's a difficult thing to understand."

"You really think you're obsessed?"

He started laughing. "What would you call it? Five or six hours a day, every day, for more than half my life? Devoting eighty, ninety, sometimes a hundred percent of my creative energy to trying to figure out how fast and how far a particular animal can run."

"I guess, when you put it like that—"

"It's my life. I can't kid even myself about that any more. The horses are my life."

I nodded.

"Don't nod," he said. "It's too easy to nod. I don't want you doing things that are easy. You understand part of it. I want you to understand it all. *I want you to know what it means.* Five hours a day, every day for twenty-five years. Do you know how lonely I get?"

"I can imagine."

"You cannot imagine! It's something else you'll have to take on faith. This is my life, kid, and I live the whole thing inside myself. Buried beneath those thousands of newspapers in my apartment. I come out every day and put on my public face and everyone says, 'Oh yeah, that Blaine, what a snide bastard he is, but I like his show,' and they don't know . . . they don't know . . . none of them knows how much I hate them and hate the show and hate myself for doing it. But I have to. I have to get out. I have to get away from the horses. At least a few hours every day I have to have something else to relate to. The strain, kid. You understand. The strain of that battle every day—trying to figure out ahead of time what will happen—it gets very hard. It gets very hard and lonely after a while."

"I can see that."

He looked at me sharply. "What do you mean?"

"I mean, you know, every day just dealing with nothing but figures."

He laughed again. "So you don't understand. Like the rest of them, you think it's just figures. It's not just figures, kid. That stuff there in the *Telegraph* is a language. I am a scholar of a language and I have devoted my life to its study."

"I never thought of it that way."

"Those figures. They might not be poetry but they're damned fine prose. Clean and pure. Simple declarative sentences. No room for bullshit on those pages. Read them, kid. You've got to read the figures like a book. The past performance charts. Numbers and abbreviations, that's all. Unless you understand. Unless you speak the language. Then they start to tell you a story. A different story every horse. Each one, kid, is a biography. A full-fledged biography right there in front of you on the page. Hundreds of them, I read hundreds of them every day."

"But they're horses. They're just biographies of horses."

"Let yourself go. Let your imagination get involved. Each one of those horses is an individual. If you under-stand his individuality, you can start to understand how he might react in the company of the other individuals he's competing with on any given day. Look at it another way. You read all the past performances that way, you've assembled the cast of characters for a play. Some major, some minor, in any particular race, but all with a part to play in the plot. The plot! That's what you've got to figure out. The characters are right there, and the setting, but you've got to figure out the plot."

Blaine's voice gradually had been getting louder. I noticed now that the few other people in the dining room were starting to stare. He stopped abruptly. "I'm going to bed, kid. Before I get carried away. This is something I haven't let myself talk about for years."

"It's interesting."

"Ah, you're like the rest of them, you only understand up to a point."

"No, no, I understand. I really do."

"I'd like to think so. I've enjoyed the conversation. But just remember, kid. Just remember." He clenched his fist and struck the table. "I did not come down here for a Florida vacation."

He leaned forward now and whispered intensely, "That track out there is where some of the biggest battles of my life have been fought. Years ago. When I still thought the outcome made a difference." He paused and took a deep breath. "I've waited twelve years, kid, to come back to this track with some dough. I've been here three days now and haven't cracked it. But I will. Remember that. *I will crack it.*"

I went to my room and lay down on the couch. I must have dozed. The phone woke me up around midnight. It was the night clerk at the desk. He spoke with a heavy

Spanish accent. He said there was a woman in the lobby, very drunk. She said she was staying with me. There was a $16 cab fare she hadn't paid. She kept yelling that I had enough money, I could pay it.

I told the clerk to pay it and put it on my bill. "And give the driver a five-dollar tip." Then I put my shoes on and went downstairs.

It was Jennifer, all right, and she was drunk. In fact, there was vomit on the front of her dress. She could barely walk and she started crying when she saw me.

"Come upstairs," I said. "What's wrong with you? What happened?"

She fell into my arms and I dragged her, almost dead weight, to the elevator. The clerk was laughing behind the desk. I guess when there are almost no guests at all in your expensive hotel, even a drunken girl can be amusing.

She cried for half an hour on the couch. I put a cold washcloth on her forehead and held her hand. Finally she told me what happened.

Sonny Holiday had never showed up. She had waited at the bar for three hours, telling everyone who would listen that she was from The Dream Team of Federated Press. Come to Florida especially to write a story about Holiday. I guess she stretched it even a little worse than that after her fourth or fifth drink, and told them all that she was famous and nominated for a Pulitzer Prize and was leaving the next week to cover the President's European tour.

And the little bastard had never showed. Jennifer had stayed at the bar, getting drunker and drunker and feeling more and more frightened and like a fool. She'd begun to cry and finally she had vomited and they'd called for the cab. The fare was so high because she had made the driver take her past the Fontainebleau and Americana before she let him bring her over to Miami.

# Thursday

BARNABY BLAINE *jerked awake from terrify-*
*ing dreams. He lay in bed, shaken by involuntary*
*muscular spasms. After a few moments he reached*
*for a cigarette. He was trembling too much to light a*
*match. Also, he was drenched with nervous sweat,*
*despite the air conditioning in the room.*

*There had been two dreams. Two dreams that he*
*had dreamed at intervals for many years. In the first,*
*all the figures in his records and charts suddenly*
*faded and blurred until they were indecipherable.*

*Like scratchings on the Rosetta Stone. For hours, in this dream, he would sit and stare at his papers, unable to distinguish even the names of the horses. This dream never reached a conclusion. It just went on and on and on. With Blaine staring at the numbers and letters that were his life; with no hope of ever knowing again what they meant.*

*In the second dream, a horse he had bet on—it was always the same horse, dark brown and powerful— began to sink deeper and deeper into the surface of the race track as it ran. The race was almost over, the horse had almost won. But now, with every stride, instead of moving forward, it sank. The surface beneath its feet would soften and melt, and first the hooves, then the legs, then the body of the horse itself would disappear. All the while the animal would struggle—desperately, in a frenzy—as if fighting for life itself. Meanwhile, on either side, the other horses in the race charged past, the track beneath their hooves as hard and tight as the surface of a drum. And, indeed, that was the sound of their hooves: a staccato drum roll, faster but of the same rhythm as a funeral march.*

*Blaine always awoke from these dreams with weak bowels. This morning was no exception. Abandoning his try to light a cigarette, he got out of bed and walked toward the darkened bathroom, tremoring once or twice on the way. He spent the first thirty minutes of his day on the toilet. Staring at the beige carpet on the bathroom floor and at the swollen blue veins of his feet.*

---

Jennifer said she had to exercise. That was the first thing she said in the morning. As if by getting an extra-fast start on the new day, she could erase all memory of the night before.

"Okay, go exercise."

"How can you stand it just lying there? You've been here four days and you haven't exercised once."

"How can you stand it? Talking about exercise with a hangover."

"Exercise makes you *feel* good."

"No. Sleep makes me feel good. Making love makes me feel good. Exercise makes me feel sick to my stomach."

"Well, I've got to exercise. I've got to sweat out my poisons in a hurry."

"So go exercise."

"Sit down and lie down. That's all we've done since I got here. Sit at the race track. Sit in the car. Sit at dinner. Sit in the room and drink. Then lie down and sleep. I need more activity than that."

"Then do something, goddamnit!" She had told me that hangovers made her aggressive, but my patience was worn pretty thin.

"Don't yell at me. Please—don't ever yell at me. That's one thing I just can't stand."

"I'm sorry. I just woke up. But look, if you want exercise, please exercise. Don't lie here and bitch."

"I'm not bitching. I never bitch. I'm simply telling you how I feel about something that's important to me. You brought me here for a week and all you've done is cart me around like a piece of baggage, never caring what I think or how I feel, just doing what you want to do all the time, never thinking about me. If you had let me go to Key West like I had wanted to, yesterday would have been a very different kind of day. Now I'm saying I have to exercise. I'm saying that my mental and physical health demand it."

"And I'm saying, Jennifer, for the fourth goddamned time—"

"Don't yell."

"I'm not yelling. I am simply raising my voice for emphasis. For the fourth goddamned time: *Exercise!*"

"Come with me."

"No."

"I can't understand people like you. You're missing so much that life has to offer."

She got up and put on a bathing suit and went to the pool. That was when I noticed it was raining. Pouring. I looked out the window to see if I could see her swimming, and I saw the rain. She was swimming anyway. In the salt-water pool. Swimming laps.

The phone rang. It was Blaine.

"Bad news."

"What is it?"

"No *Telegraphs* downtown at five A.M. I've got to go back. Want to come?"

"Sure."

"You'd better think twice. Have you been out yet?"

"No, but I see it's raining."

"Yeah, and the temperature at eight o'clock was fifty-two degrees."

"Oh my God. And Jennifer's swimming."

"What?"

"She's swimming. In the pool. You can see her out your window."

"What the hell is she doing that for?"

"She said she needed exercise."

"How did her interview go?"

"Oh, Jesus, Barnaby. Don't mention it. Whatever you do, don't ask her. That little shit Holiday stood her up."

She came back just as I was ready to leave. Shivering, and dripping water on the thick blue rug.

"How was it?"

"Fantastic!"

"Barnaby says it's fifty-two degrees outside."

"I love to swim in the cold."

"I watched you out the window."

"Why didn't you come down?"

"How many laps did you swim?"

"Twenty. Then I rested awhile and did ten more. God, I feel marvelous." She jumped about five feet across the room.

I told her I was going downtown to get the *Telegraph*s. She said she was going to take a shower.

"Just remember the one and only rule of the house," I said. "Don't answer the phone."

I turned to wink at her as I walked out the door. But

instead of smiling, as she had been, she was standing with her hands on her hips, her mouth open, and a curious, shocked expression on her face.

She was on the phone when I came back. Talking to her roommate in San Francisco.

"No, at night we just sit around and drink," she was saying.

She talked for fifteen minutes while I looked at the *Telegraph.* Joie de Vivre and Sea Change had both been officially entered in the Flamingo. Jennifer kept asking about who was at the party Saturday night and did Donald like Liz's new hairstyle and was Hank drinking much and who stayed over and what did they do Sunday, and finally I went into the bedroom and closed the door.

"God, I miss that kid," Jennifer said when she came in.

"Who?"

"Patsy. My roommate."

"You've only been away from her for four days."

"Yes, but we're really close."

"You talked long enough. How long were you on before I got here?"

"Maybe ten minutes. What's the big deal?"

"No big deal. You called her, I assume."

"Of course. *Since I'm not allowed to answer the phone.*"

"Did you call collect?"

"No, I didn't call collect."

"Oh."

"Why?"

"That's not cheap, you know. Half an hour to San Francisco."

"God, you're amazing."

"Why am I amazing?"

"All the money you spent to bring me here. All the money you bet on a stupid bunch of horses. And you complain because I make one call to my roommate."

"I'm not complaining, Jennifer, but I'm a little surprised that you would just pick up the phone and do that."

"How can you be so cheap?"

"It's not a question of being cheap. But I think you might have asked me first. And I wonder, again, why you have to talk to your roommate for half an hour when you've only been away four days."

"I told you. We're very close." She went back to the living room and slammed the door behind her.

Jennifer sat between us, a sketchbook in her lap. She was going to make drawings at the track today, and pretend she'd never heard of Sonny Holiday. She said she found sketching therapeutic. The car windows were shut tight against the rain.

The windshield kept fogging up. Blaine wiped it with the edge of his hand and left streaks. His breath smelled awful, as if he had been poisoned the night before. The odor filled the car. There was no way to let it out. The rain came down so hard, we could not drive over forty on the expressway. Already my shirt was soaked with sweat. More sweat dripped down my forehead and the sides of my face. Blaine wiped the inside of the windshield again. The day was so dark we had our lights on. Jennifer pushed the radio buttons but all she got were commercials.

"Why don't you turn that off, sweetie," Blaine said.

She snapped it off. Not saying a word. Blaine exhaled. The windshield fogged up again.

We had no umbrella. Who would bring an umbrella to a week at Hialeah?

"Why don't you have an umbrella?" Jennifer asked.

"We don't need one."

"How are we going to get from the parking lot to the track?" she said. "Is someone going to dig us a tunnel?"

Blaine got on the valet parking line. For $2.50 a guy in an orange cap will park your car. The advantage is you get out right at the entrance to the clubhouse. Even at noon there were about six hundred cars ahead of us on the line. We sat, moving forward inches at a time, for twenty minutes. We perspired.

"If we had umbrellas we wouldn't have to do this," Jennifer said. "We could have parked where we've parked all week. We could be inside by now."

Blaine said he thought we should have a drink together to celebrate what he called "our imminent recovery." Jennifer had a bloody mary. I had a screwdriver. Blaine had a triple bourbon on the rocks. I noticed that his hands were shaking badly.

"Today," he said "we make up for what's been happening this week. Today we have six horses to bet. The drought is over. Our patience is about to pay off."

I hoped he was right. I had sat calmly through three days, but now all at once I was realizing that I was $700 in the hole—money that would have to be paid back— and there were only three days left until we went home.

One thing Blaine was right about: the drought. It had been over for three days now. But today was the worst. Pouring rain, almost violent; by far, the hardest of the week.

We watched the first race, in which we had no bet. It was at six furlongs, but before the horses even got to the turn, all except the leader were covered with mud and it was impossible to tell them apart. The surface of the track was under water. The hooves of the horses would splash through this water and into the slop below and big pieces of it would fly up and cover the horses and jockeys in the rear. The race was won by a horse that paid $26. The 6–5 favorite finished seventh.

"They're so dumb," Blaine said. "So dumb. They never learn."

"Who are so dumb?" Jennifer said.

"People. They threw money on that horse like it was a stakes winner, and it's a crummy five-thousand-dollar claimer."

"You're full of contempt, aren't you?"

"For stupidity, yes."

"But they're people. Just because they don't know as much about horse racing as you do is no reason to be contemptuous. They've got problems. Hopes, fears, dignity. And—"

"What is this, Sunday School?"

"No, but it bothers me to see you—to see the two of you—sit here feeling so superior. I hate condescension.

It's unchristian. It's dehumanizing. And you two are as guilty of it as any two people I've ever seen."

"If we're offending you that terribly, sweetheart, you can climb into a cab and go back to the hotel. We're here to bet horses. This isn't Don McNeil's Breakfast Club."

"And if you don't leave, Jennifer, goddamnit, you'd just goddamn well better keep your mouth shut." I was so mad I couldn't sit. I got up for a beer.

When I came back, bringing one for Blaine, Jennifer was gone.

"Did she go back to the hotel?"

Blaine shrugged. "As soon as you left she said excuse me and walked away. Maybe she went to the john."

In the second race we bet a horse named Bushel 'n' Peck at 5–2. This would cut my loss in half. The next one would get me even. Bushel 'n' Peck was starting from post position 12, on the far outside, and had lots of early speed. It was perfect. By starting from outside, he could stay clear of all the slop that the others would kick around. With early speed, and the long run to the turn that seven-furlong races have, he would be able to get the lead easily. Holiday was riding; he could win without getting even a dirty face.

The rain fell harder. Bushel 'n' Peck broke quickly from the gate, but so did two horses on the inside. At the turn they were still inside him, forcing Holiday wide. He passed them, finally, but had used his horse so hard that he had little left for the stretch. Nobody else had much either, and for a moment I thought we still might win. Then a 25–1 shot called Trapeze Tony swept by us at the

144

wire. The photo-finish sign went up, but I knew we had lost. By a head. By the length of a horse's head.

For the first time all week I felt scared. "We can't buy a break."

Blaine was silent.

"I mean . . . Trapeze Tony."

He still was silent.

"Shit."

I noticed a muscle in the side of his face begin to twitch.

"That horse ran tenth, beaten seventeen lengths his last time out. Against the same class of horses. Hadn't won a race in ten months. What kind of shit is this?"

"Stop whimpering," Blaine said. Then he put a cigarette between trembling lips.

We did not bet the third or fourth. We sat and watched the rain. Jennifer did not come back. I thought she might have gone to the publicity office to complain about Holiday not showing up. Although that could only have increased her humiliation. Then I thought maybe she had gone back to the hotel.

No matter where she was, I did not want to see her for a while. All I wanted to do was win a race. This was getting ridiculous. A week at Hialeah with one of the outstanding handicappers of horses in America and it was Thursday afternoon and I had not cashed a bet.

We had a horse called Corn Cob Pipe in the fifth. Holiday, again, was the rider. He was due to win. Almost as due as we were. He had ridden losers in each of the first four races, plus the tenth the day before. Served him right. If it had been up to me, I wouldn't have bet the little shit again all week. But Corn Cob Pipe was at the top of Blaine's figures. And Blaine's figures were all we had.

"Shall we go down and look at him?"

Blaine shook his head. "Not in this rain. His ankles would be under water anyway. This is an allowance race, pretty good class of horses. We'll watch him through the glasses when he comes out. If he's not limping, he's a bet."

He was not limping. He was a bet. He finished third. I was out $900 for the week.

From there it got worse in a hurry. We lost on a horse named Foley, at 7–2, in the sixth; and on Thirty Day Fast, at 8–5, in the seventh, and win and place bets on a 5–1 horse whose name I forget in the eighth. And on an even-money favorite in the ninth. Blaine and I had not spoken for two hours. We would sit in silence until five minutes before the race. Then he would point to the name of a horse in his program. We would walk together, in silence, to the $100 window. I allowed him to bet first. Then we would walk, still silent, not even looking at each other, back to our seats.

I was out $1,400 for the week. I had lost fourteen consecutive bets. For the past three races our horses hadn't even been close. Jennifer was still gone but I had not thought about her for an hour and a half. This whole thing was happening much too fast. Okay, we had lost a few bets the first couple of days. And then drawn a blank on the third. That kind of thing happened. Sixty percent losers, Blaine had said, even with all of his caution. But I had lost fourteen consecutive bets! I could win seven in a row now and still not achieve forty percent winners for the week. And Jesus, there was no reason to think I would win the next seven bets in a row.

My mind had gone numb. I was acting mechanically. The fog in my head was growing thick as the fog around the track. It occurred to me once to get drunk. If I got drunk in a real hurry, I would not be so conscious of this. But no. To get drunk would be to give up. And I couldn't give up. I was with Barnaby Blaine. And his Rain Manual and his slide rules and his magnifying glass and his obsession. And the 13,176 *Racing Forms* and *Morning Telegraphs* that filled up his apartment in San Francisco.

"This rain," I said, as we sat dumbly in our seats, waiting for the horses to come onto the track for the last race of the day. "This rain must have something to do with it. Maybe it's throwing the figures off."

"Shut up!" Blaine hissed. "What the *fuck* do you think I've spent twenty years compiling a Rain Manual for?"

"I don't know. I'm just looking for a reason."

"The condition of the track has never affected the validity of the figures. I've checked that out specifically time and again. For years. For years, understand?"

"Okay, so it's not the rain. What is it?"

"I don't know."

He said it very quietly. Looking not at me but at the sodden flamingos in the infield, and the rain falling into the lake.

Jennifer came back. I had just made my bet for the tenth: a horse called Sad State—$100 win, $100 place. The price was 8–1 and he was the top horse in Blaine's figures by the largest margin of the day. It looked too good to be true. And it's a good name, I was telling myself. I've got that much extra going. A good name for the condition we're in.

I was walking down the steps toward our seats when I saw her. I had stopped at the men's room and Blaine had gone ahead. She was with him at the seats, squeezing his shoulder and grinning.

"Oooooh. Barnaby says you've been losing."

"Where have you been?"

"Isn't that funny? Barnaby asked the same question."

"Jennifer, where the fuck have you been?"

She gave me one of those hurt looks, as though I had wounded her with my language. As if she didn't moan the word all over the bedroom floor at night.

"I just told Barnaby. I needed some time by myself."

"Where were you?"

"Around. Making sketches."

"Of what?"

"Of some of the people that you think you're too good to talk to."

Just then the last of the horses went into the gate and the track announcer said, "It is now post time," and I forgot about her. Stopped trying to figure what had made her such a bitch from the moment she woke up. Forgot about the bad feelings that were eating the day away, leaving us tired and raw. Forgot, almost, that if Sad State lost, I would be $1,600 behind.

I picked up my binoculars and my heart started to pound the way it does before every race I ever have made a bet on, whether it is $2 or $100. My hands shook slightly as I held the glasses, peering through the rain at the starting gate, which was just up the track from us, on our side because the race was a mile and an eighth.

Jesus, I wanted to win this. I deserved to. And what about Blaine? The poor man. He was suffering not only from losing money—I had no idea how much—but from having this all happen after finally dropping the mask a little bit. After sharing the big secret about how the horses were really all that mattered in his life.

He sat next to me now. Sweat pouring off him. Hands shaking so badly he could not hold the glasses too close to his eyes without running the risk of detaching a retina. Twenty-five years of his life. Adding up to little numbers and letters, written on an index card, with the ink now blurring in the rain.

Sad State.

It sure as hell was.

There were ten horses in the race. Sad State was starting from the outside post position. There was very little straight track before the first turn, which meant the jockey would have to either take the turn on the outside—if he moved Sad State toward the front of the field—or pull back along the rail behind most of the other horses.

Ordinarily, this was no problem. Coming off the turn he

would have the full backstretch—almost three-eighths of a mile—in which to move his horse. Then another turn, and then the homestretch, a quarter-mile more.

But with the track in such terrible condition, with water and slippery mud splashing everywhere, it would not be good to get caught behind a lot of horses. Early speed has a tradition of holding up on sloppy tracks, even in longer races. And this was as sloppy a track as I had ever seen.

Sad State did go for the lead. He broke so well from the gate that he almost got it, too. A 15–1 horse named Booster Rocket moved to the lead on the rail. Sad State, cutting in front of the field, fell into stride alongside. The favorite, Nutty Putty, was back in the pack. So was Dover Beach, the second choice, the horse that Sonny Holiday rode.

Booster Rocket stayed in front down the backstretch. Sad State held second place, never more than two lengths behind. On the turn, Booster Rocket tired. Sad State's jockey moved him immediately to the outside, passed Booster Rocket, and came back inside with a length-and-a-half lead.

Nobody else was moving. Nutty Putty and Holiday's horse, Dover Beach, were lost in the muddy pack.

"Barnaby!"

"It's a long stretch."

"Yeah, but he's pulling away."

"Three lengths ahead now. Four."

Blaine and I were watching through our binoculars. We had rented a pair for Jennifer but she wasn't using them.

"We're a winner!"

"He's all by himself."

At 8–1, with a decent place price, I could make almost $1,500 profit on the race.

"We made it, Barnaby! We're winners for the trip!" I put my binoculars down. The field was splashing toward the finish, just a sixteenth of a mile away, with Sad State still four lengths ahead.

"We're winners! We're winners!" I was so happy I even squeezed Jennifer's arm.

"*Wait!*"

Blaine still had his binoculars on the field.

"What?"

"Look!"

I looked back at the track just in time to see the finish. In which two horses—Sad State and another that was covered by mud—swept past the finish line together.

"Who was that? Where did he come from?"

Blaine put down his glasses. His face was pale and he seemed about to convulse. "Dover Beach," he said. "He came out of a cannon."

"He didn't catch us, did he?"

"I don't know. We're at a bad angle here for judging finishes. If he didn't he didn't miss by much."

The photo sign was up. The electric red of the word PHOTO glowing through the rain and dark.

"Oh, Jesus." Dover Beach. With Sonny Holiday the jockey.

Blaine lit a cigarette.

"Give me one."

It trembled in my lips. Fifteen hundred dollars if the place price was good. Ahead for the trip. PHOTO. Glowing—burning now as if some kind of evil branding iron. Christ, how long does it take to look at a picture? What are they doing up there?

I stared at the blank spaces where the numbers would go when the judges determined from the picture who had won. Sad State was number 12. Dover Beach was 4.

I could see it. Very clearly I could see it in my mind:

12

4

I would run to the window, cheering, and get my money. And be ahead for the trip. And have the next two days to build a profit. Plenty of time, really. Hell, a couple more winners like this? I would drink champagne and fall in love with Jennifer and even bring a present home to my wife. *Just put the fucking numbers up.*

4

12

9

1

They all went up at once. The order of finish of the first four horses.

"Jesus fucking Christ," Blaine whispered.

"Oooooh," Jennifer squealed. "You lost."

I sucked in my breath and turned toward the stairs that led to the cashier's window. We still had place bets to collect. I threw my cigarette away. I wanted to punch something. Somebody. The board with the numbers on it. A horse. A jockey. Jennifer. Blaine. My stomach quivered;

every muscle in my body trembled. Then I felt as if I was going to cry.

They had a rerun on videotape, the way that have at all the good tracks now. I made myself watch it. The whole thing.

"Come on," Blaine said. "Let's get out of here. That won't do any good."

But I still could not believe it. I had to see it. Here it was again, around the turn, into the stretch, Sad State ahead by two, three, four lengths, and holding at four. There was nothing else even in the picture.

Then suddenly—it was shocking, even though I knew it was going to happen—there came a horse faster than I've ever seen a horse come. On the outside. Covered with mud, with Holiday whipping so fast I could not follow the motion of his arm.

I turned away. I knew how it came out. Sad State only paid $4.80 to place. I got back $240 for the $200 I had bet altogether, which left me down $660 for the day and $1,360 for the trip.

"Let's go," Blaine said. "It'll take us an hour to get the goddamned car."

"Just a minute." Jennifer spoke in a shrill, crowing voice. "Just one minute, boys."

As we watched, she reached into her pocketbook and extracted a pari-mutuel ticket. It was a $10 win ticket on a number 4 horse, but I could not tell for which race.

"What is that?" I said. Blaine said nothing. He just stared, his mouth slightly open.

"This," Jennifer said, holding it closer so I could see it clearly, "is a winning ticket. At least that's what it looks like to my inexpert eyes. Heehee. Dover Beach. Ten dollars to win. Now tell me where I collect."

"Jennifer, what did you—?"

"Sorry, boys. But I gave you almost four full days to prove yourselves. And you were not able to do it. So I decided to use a little woman's intuition. I bet on Sonny Holiday."

"Jennifer, how could you!"

"Simple. He's obviously the hottest jockey at the track, so he's obviously got the best chance to win. I told you that a couple of days ago."

"But . . . but . . . and especially after last night."

"What does last night have to do with the price of eggs? You can't let emotion influence your judgment. That's what Barnaby always says. I decided that Sonny was the best jockey and so I decided to bet on him. After that, it was just a question of waiting for the right horse. When I saw Dover Beach, I knew I couldn't lose. I just *adore* Matthew Arnold."

I looked around for Blaine. He was not there any more. Then I saw the back of his raincoat disappear through the doorway that led to the crowd of people waiting for their cars. Even from a distance I could see how his shoulders were stooped.

Jennifer giggled. "Come on. If you're not going to

congratulate me, at least point me in the right direction to collect."

Not saying a word, I turned and hurried after Blaine.

We had to wait twenty-five minutes beneath the green and white awning for the car. I stood by myself, my hands in my raincoat pocket, staring at the ground. Blaine stood by himself, his arms folded, staring at the top of the awning. Jennifer circulated among small groups of strangers, grinning and giggling, and telling people, a little too loudly, I thought, what a thrill it was to have won her first bet at a race track, *especially when she picked out the horse all by herself.*

"Car's here," Blaine said. "You drive."

"How come?"

He held out his hands. They were trembling as if incurably diseased.

I ran around to the driver's side in the rain, tipped the man in the orange cap a dollar, and we drove back to the hotel with the radio on, hearing "Bridge Over Troubled Waters" twice.

"I just want to say one thing," Jennifer said. "You're not going to like it, but I'm going to say it anyway because it's something you ought to hear. For your own good."

"Say it. Don't give it a fifteen-minute introduction. Say it."

We were in the hotel room. Drying out. Gray outside, rain still falling.

"You're a sore loser."

"Say that again."

"You're the sorest loser I've ever seen. You're spoiled. You're a baby."

I had control of myself. I had complete control of myself. I wasn't going to shout.

"What makes you say that?" I had such control of myself, I was whispering.

"The way you're acting now. The way you've acted since you lost that race."

"Jennifer, I happen to be a very good loser. All I've done is brood. Sore losers beat up people after races like that. They go to the men's room and slash their wrists."

"But you don't have a right to brood. If you can't afford to lose, you shouldn't bet. If you don't know how to lose, you shouldn't bet. And you must not know how, because you certainly can afford it."

"Jennifer, that's not the point. The money has nothing to do with it. The money doesn't matter."

"Hah!"

"It doesn't, for Christ's sake! You don't understand anything about playing horses. It's not the money. It's the idea. From the day I reached the age of reason, all I've heard is how you can't beat the horses. You can beat a race but you can't beat the races. I think it was printed in my first-grade catechism.

"Well, goddamn it, you can beat the races! You can beat them day after day, year after year. And Barnaby Blaine has done it.

"He's worked for twenty-five years to perfect his method. And he's succeeded. You've heard him say so yourself. That's what pisses me off. It's not losing a thousand dollars. It's that there's no reason for this to be happening! That's why I brood. That's why I'm shouting now. *Because there's not one fucking reason in the world for us not to be ahead!*"

"Ugly."

"What?"

"Sometimes you're very ugly."

"Jennifer, get out of here."

"And you're still not being honest with yourself. That's all I want. I want you to be honest with yourself. I don't even care if you're a sore loser. I don't care if you're cheap. I just want you to be honest with yourself. If I could teach you that one ability, I'd consider this week a success."

"Jennifer, get out of here. Go somewhere so I don't have to look at you. *Fast!*"

"You can't take it, can you? You can't take a mirror held up to your face."

"Jennifer, I swear to God the next thing I'm going to do is slap you across the mouth."

"Can't take it. Can't take the truth."

"*Get out of here!*"

"A sore loser who can't take the truth." She turned and walked toward the door. But at the door she stopped and turned again. "And cheap, too. A thousand dollars on horses but you can't spend fifty for a phonograph and a couple of records so we could have music in the room at night. A phonograph? Hah! You didn't even bring a radio."

She went out the door. There was a half-full bottle of Scotch on a table near where I was standing. I picked it up and threw it. As hard as I could. Toward the door. It smashed against a wall, spraying glass and Scotch over half the room. I went into the bedroom and counted the money I had left. Six hundred dollars. I waited ten minutes until I was calm. Then I went down to the cocktail lounge.

Blaine had his hands folded in front of him on the table. Jennifer had one of hers on top of them. She was stroking lightly and smiling at him while he talked. She wore a white linen dress with yellow ribbons in it, and had a yellow ribbon in her hair. She looked very pretty, and I hated her guts.

A martini was waiting for me. I stood by the table and drank it in two gulps. Then I inhaled deeply and sat down.

Blaine looked at Jennifer. "I think you're right," he said.

"You think she's right about what?"

He looked at me. "You are a sore loser."

"What—"

"Nnnnyah," Jennifer said, and stuck her tongue out at me. "I've been telling Barnaby how badly you've been treating me."

"And we've decided you've been taking her for granted. We think she deserves a better man. One with the maturity to appreciate her."

"Like you, lover," she said, pinching Blaine's cheek. "Grrrr."

Then they both burst out laughing. I could see it was going to be a very jolly night. I was puzzled at first by how nice Blaine was being to Jennifer. Then I realized he was doing it to punish himself.

She stood and walked around the table and stuck her tongue in my ear. She said, "Even with all of your faults, I think you're pretty nice."

I said I would have another drink.

Dinner was awful again. In the hotel. I had steak with some kind of pâté on top of it. The pâté was cold and looked as if one of the horses had dropped it on the track. We drank three bottles of wine instead of two. Blaine ordered lamb chops but left them untouched. They lay on his plate cold and gray—like dead sparrows.

By the end of the meal Jennifer was restless again. "Let's do something tonight."

"I thought you did something last night," Blaine said. He was not being so nice to her any more.

She ignored him. "I mean something fun."

"Fun!" I said. "I lost almost seven hundred dollars today."

"Five percent," Blaine said. "That wouldn't have happened if you'd only been betting five percent."

"But I thought we were going to win. Last night you told me we would win. This morning you told me we would win."

"We will. We'll win tomorrow. That's why you shouldn't have been betting so much today."

"Stop!" Jennifer said. "I'm sick of this incessant conversation about the race track. It's bad enough you spend all day out there in the rain and don't win. But now you've got to come back here and talk about it all night. I'm telling you both, I can't stand it any more and I want to be shown a good time. I think that's the least I have a right to expect."

"What do you want to do, Jennifer? Go to a nightclub?" I said.

"I wouldn't mind dancing."

"No. Every place around here is a clip joint. I'm not going to blow fifty bucks in a Miami Beach hotel just to hear some 1940's music."

"Well—"

"And don't start that cheapskate shit again. I don't mind spending money if it's fun. Miami Beach night life is not fun."

"Sitting in a hotel room feeling sorry for yourself is fun?"

"It's as good as anything else."

"I wouldn't mind staying in—even without music—if we only had something to do." She paused for a moment, thinking. Blaine and I drank the last of our wine.

"If we only had a dartboard."

"A dartboard!"

"Yes. I love to play darts."

Blaine chuckled. "Forget the board, sweetie. Just give me the darts and I'll bring them to the track tomorrow. I can think of a few animals I wouldn't mind throwing them at." He laughed a little louder.

"I'm serious. Do you think the hotel has a dartboard?"

Then I started to laugh. I couldn't help it. People at other tables began to stare.

"It's not so funny," Jennifer said. "In San Francisco I play darts all the time. Patsy and I stay home for nights at a time playing darts."

"Jennifer, you're too much."

"Well, you're so inactive it makes me sick. Both of you. Sit and drink. Sit and talk. Sit and look at horses. Life is passing you by. You've got to get in the swim. You've got to come alive. It's just like my high school gym teacher used to say: the world is spinning—spin with it."

Blaine and I were both still laughing. "Come alive?" I managed to say. "By playing darts?"

"By doing something. Darts were just an example. I have a better idea. We won't need any equipment at all. We'll play charades."

That did it. Blaine and I broke up completely. The headwaiter finally came over to ask if we wanted anything else.

"Charades!" Blaine gasped. "Beautiful. I could pose as a horse-racing expert." He was laughing so hard he had to put his head down on the table.

"I'd like to be excused," Jennifer said, not smiling. "I'll be waiting in the lobby."

She tried once more. We went to my room and I poured Scotch for all of us from a bottle I had not broken. Blaine and I sat on the couch. Jennifer stood and started to make motions with her hands.

"Here's a clue," she said. "It's the title of a best-selling

161

novel." She held up one finger. Then she lay on her back on the floor and started to move her legs in a bicycling motion.

Blaine sat silently, staring at her crotch.

"Jennifer," I said. "Please get up off the floor. We don't want to play."

She stopped, with less fuss than I expected, but she would not talk to us. She took her notebook from her bag and sat off in a corner, writing in it. Blaine and I talked horses. We planned our comeback, and figured how much money we could reasonably expect to make in two days.

Finally I said, "What are you doing, Jennifer? Writing poetry?"

"Drawing sketches."

"Of what?"

"Of Barnaby."

"Why Barnaby?"

"Because, despite everything, he's got an eloquent face."

I thought about this for a moment. Then I said, "And I don't?"

"No. Your face is just something to look at. Barnaby's face is like the reading of a psalm. It speaks to me. It speaks of places he's been and places he still wants to go. The eyes, the tilt of the nose, the sag of the jowl—"

"The rupture of the blood vessels in the cheeks," Blaine said. Then he got up to go to the bathroom.

When he came back Jennifer said she had two sketches completed. She walked across the room to show them to us. In each, Blaine looked like Paul Newman. This was a resemblance I had not detected before.

"These aren't sketches of Barnaby," I said. "These are sketches of Paul Newman."

"You know nothing, absolutely nothing, about art," Blaine said. "I think she's captured my essence."

"I wanted your integrity to show," she said. Then she went back to her corner and started to draw again.

This time it was a wristwatch with a peace symbol formed by the position of the hands.

"A friend of mine in San Francisco wants to market these," she said. "I think it's a beautiful idea."

"Except," I said, "the only times the hands are in the right position are five thirty-five and seven twenty-five. What about the rest of the day?"

"The hands never move. The face revolves instead. The hands always point toward peace. It's very symbolic."

She paused, waiting for Blaine or me to say something. Neither of us did.

"I think it's beautiful," she said. "The first time he explained it to me, he made me cry."

The phone rang. It was the front desk.

"We have a special delivery package for you, sir. Would you like us to send it up?"

"A special delivery package?"

Jennifer jumped from her chair. "The grass!" she yelled. "The grass! Patsy sent the grass!"

"Yes," I said, "send it up."

A bellman was there in five minutes. The package was square, wrapped in plain brown paper, with no return address. My name and address were printed clumsily, as if by a child. Inside the package was a man's shaving kit.

163

"Oh, that Patsy. She's such a trickster," Jennifer said. "She's given us a treasure hunt."

I unzipped the shaving kit and, one by one, put the contents on the imitation-marble-topped coffee table.

—A Gillette adjustable razor, set at number seven.

—A five-pack of Gillette super stainless blades with one blade left. And no blades in the used-blade receptacle in the back.

—A half-full tube of Crest toothpaste which had not been rolled up from the bottom.

—A soft yellow toothbrush with bristles sticking out in all directions.

—A can of Rise shaving cream. Plain, not menthol.

—A silver can of Right Guard deodorant.

—Small bottles of Old Spice after-shave lotion and cologne and a slightly rusty can of Old Spice talcum.

—A LaCroix nail clipper.

—A greasy military hairbrush, with strands of graying hair weaved through it.

"That must be Buster's shaving kit," Jennifer said. "Buster is Patsy's old boyfriend."

I tried the toothpaste first, slicing the tube open with the one razor blade. There was only toothpaste inside. The Old Spice bottles did not seem promising, but the talcum did. I pried off the top and poured talcum powder — plain talcum powder—all over the table.

That meant it was either the deodorant or the shaving cream. The shaving cream can was bigger, so I tried it first. The top was intact, but when I pulled at the bottom, it was loose, held on by a heavy glue. I pulled harder. Slowly, stickily, it gave way.

Inside the can, instead of shaving cream, there was a lump of what looked like Saran Wrap, compressed tightly by about a dozen thin rubber bands. I took off the rubber bands and unfolded the Saran Wrap. Inside, shaped into a cylinder by three more rubber bands, were at least a dozen cigarettes.

I counted. Eighteen. Thick and packed tight.

I smelled. Strong and pure.

"What an angel," Jennifer said. "She must have stayed home all day Sunday and rolled them."

"Let's go, let's go," Jennifer said. "Let's light up." She had put her notebook away and was running around the room now as if her dress were on fire. "Let's each smoke a whole one," she said. "Instead of passing it around."

I said something about the communal spirit but Jennifer said she just wanted to get stoned.

"All right, I've inhaled a lungful of the shit. What next?"

"Oh, noooo, Barnaby. You can't just inhale it. You've got to *suck* it into your lungs. Sharp. Fast." She jumped out of her chair. "*Sssuck. Sssssuck.*" She demonstrated. "And then when you've got it there, you've got to hold it. Try counting to yourself. Count to five before you let it out. One hippopotamus . . . two hippopotamus . . ."

Blaine coughed and turned purple.

"Jennifer, for Christ's sake. Let the man smoke a cigarette. We've got enough here so the maid will get wiped out just breathing the air in the morning."

"That's not the point. There is a right way to do this

and a wrong way. And that's one thing I believe. No matter what kind of endeavor it is. If it is worth doing at all, it is worth doing right."

"Is that something else your high school gym teacher told you?"

She turned her back to me and started to go through the whole business again with Blaine. I got up to go to the bathroom. Even from there I could hear her saying, "Three hippopotamus, four . . ."

"You sure I'll be able to tell I'm not just drunk?" Blaine said.

"Absolutely," Jennifer said. "Especially with this much. If you don't feel anything after the first one, just smoke another. But wow, this is strong. This is good. It won't take much." She inhaled deeply. "Wow, man, far out."

"Oh, fuck you, Jennifer."

"What?"

"I said fuck you. Stop talking like a Haight-Ashbury fifteen-year-old. 'Wow, man, far out.'"

She got out of her chair and walked to where I was sitting and dug her fingernails into my wrist as hard as she could. "Let me be myself," she said. "Let me be me."

"Goddamnit. That hurts."

"I've got a soul," she said, "in case you haven't noticed. I've got an individual identity. And I consider that the flowering of this identity is something sacred. Don't try to cast a shadow over me."

There came a terrible racking cough from Blaine's

chair. His eyes were watering and he gasped for breath. "Christ," he said. "Wood alcohol is easier to consume."

Jennifer let go of my wrist and went back to minister to him. There were deep, pale crescents where her finger-nails had been.

"Suck it in. *Sssuck* it in. And hold it. That's it. Hippopotamus. Oh, Barnaby." She suddenly threw her arms around him and kissed him on the lips. "Wait until I tell everyone back home that I turned on Barnaby Blaine for the first time in his life."

My mouth was dry, so I went to the refrigerator for a beer.

"God," Jennifer said. "I wish we had music. You really need music, Barnaby, to turn on right."

We were on our second now and I could tell that I was not just drunk.

"Just think. Just think of Jimi Hendrix now, or the Doors, or Iron Butterfly. Oh God, God." And she started to pull at her hair.

"I hate them all," I said. "And Barnaby would hate them worse."

"Have you ever listened to them stoned?" she demanded.

"Not that I remember. But anybody you have to be stoned to listen to, I don't want to hear."

"You really don't know where it's at."

"Jennifer, stop talking like a cartoon."

"I feel a little tingly," Blaine said. "Are you supposed to feel tingly?"

Somebody laughed.

I heard Blaine say, "Hey, you're feeling it." His voice seemed to be coming from far away. The words took a long time to reach me.

Then I realized that I was the one who had been laughing.

We were on our third now, smoking as if they were plain cigarettes.

"The stars are dancing," Jennifer announced from the window. "The stars are doing a ballet." She tried to pirouette across the room but bumped into the coffee table and got talcum powder on her dress.

"Hey, I feel very tingly now. I'm tingling all over. Am I supposed to be tingling all over?"

"Once I made love to a black. Did you know that?" Jennifer was on her knees, holding my hand. "Do you know that once I made love to a black?"

"Yes," I said. "I know."

"How do you know?"

"You just told me."

"Well?"

"Well, what?"

"Aren't you going to ask me how it was?"

"No. I'm not."

She took a long drag from her cigarette. Her eyes were

very bloodshot. "A religious experience," she said. "It was a religious experience."

"Tingle . . . tingle . . . tingle," Blaine said from across the room. "I'm tingling softly, like a bell."

"Where's Jennifer?"

"In the bedroom."

I had gone to the bathroom and when I came back she was gone. I wondered what she was doing in the bedroom. Then I realized I could open the door and find out.

She was lying on her bed, talking on the telephone.

"Don't worry," she said. "I didn't answer it."

I had no idea what she meant. I closed the door and went back to Blaine.

"Let's smoke another," he said.

"I don't think I can."

"Come on, come on. Why quit now?"

"I don't feel so good."

"At least split one with me."

"Okay. I guess I owe you that much."

"Owe me that much for what?"

"For letting me spend this week with you."

But I could only take two drags from the cigarette. I was starting to feel very sick. We sat for a long time, Blaine talking, but me too sick to even listen. I knew I could not sit up much longer. Blaine stopped talking for a while and I could hear Jennifer's voice from the bedroom.

It sounded as if she was crying. I wondered why she had been on the phone for so long.

Jennifer came out of the bedroom.

"I said I didn't answer it."

At first I didn't realize she was screaming.

"I SAID I DIDN'T ANSWER IT!"

She was screaming. I looked at her, trying to figure out why.

She started to laugh. Then she walked to Blaine and fell into his lap and started to cry. "God, I miss Patsy. God, I love her."

She stopped sobbing long enough to look at me. "She cares about me. She cares what happens to me. She wants what's best for me."

Then she put her head on Blaine's shoulder and started to cry again. I could not figure out why. It must mean something profound. She had been screaming. I was sure of that. At least the second time. But already I had forgotten what it was that she had screamed. I was about to ask her—just out of curiosity—when the phone rang.

I wobbled and felt as if I was going to be sick when I stood up. Nobody else seemed to hear the phone. Jennifer was sobbing and Blaine was rubbing her neck. That much I was sure of. That much I could see. But I didn't know why. I did know that I had to answer the phone. I went to the bedroom to do it. Not because it would be quieter. Because I could lie on the bed. I had to lie down. Right away.

170

I picked up the phone. The receiver was very heavy. Too heavy to hold. I hung up and lay flat on the bed.

Again. The phone was ringing. I was lying on the bed. The room was dark. I was lying on my back. I reached out and felt the receiver. I was going to throw up if I moved any part of my body other than my right arm. I was going to throw up anyway. I knew that. But maybe I wouldn't throw up until after I answered the phone.

"H'lo."

"Hello? Hello? Are you all right? Why did you just hang up?" It was my wife.

"'M fine."

"You don't sound fine. Are you sick? Are you drunk? What's going on down there?"

"Nothin'. I . . . am . . . fine."

"Oh God. Why . . . why . . ." Then she started to cry.

"Hey," I said. Speaking with great difficulty. "Stop."

"Please, please, *please* come home. Please, at least give us a chance."

"Right. I will. I . . . promise. I'll call . . ." I wanted to say "tomorrow" but I couldn't. Too many syllables. "I'll call soon."

I hung up. I was sick. My only decision was whether getting to the bathroom was worth the effort it would take. It seemed much easier to simply throw up off the side of the bed. Suddenly sweat gushed out of me and I felt myself fainting and vomiting all at once. I fell off the bed and crawled to the bathroom, and hanging over the toilet bowl, vomited and vomited and vomited in the dark. From very far away, I thought I could hear Jennifer screaming.

I was lying on the bed again. I didn't know how I had got there. The room was dark. Somebody else was in it. Jennifer. She was unbuttoning my shirt. I reached out to touch her. She was naked.

"Jennifer?"

She didn't say anything. She unzipped my pants and started to pull them off. My shoes and socks already were off. I still felt sick. I felt like throwing up again and I could feel myself sweat and I felt too weak to even talk to her. She pulled my arms out of my shirt. Then she lay down on top of me and started to kiss me. Only she wasn't just kissing. She was biting my lips. Hard. It hurt. She started to bite my cheeks. She was squeezing my arms. Hard. I could feel her fingernails digging. My stomach felt awful and I was so weak.

"Hey."

Still she said nothing. She began to kiss my body and bite it, working her way down my neck and chest, biting my nipples, which hurt. Then my stomach and then skipping to my thighs and gripping the insides of them with her teeth, and sucking. I could feel her sucking, and working her way up.

Then I heard her crying.

"Jennifer?"

She started to do other things. Many other things. Including a few things I had never had done to me before.

Using her hands, lips, tongue, teeth, nose. Using them everywhere. Begging for a response. There was none. I was limp and cold and sick.

She straightened up and knelt above me.

"Jennifer, I'm sick. Please leave me alone."

Instead she started to work with her hands. Furiously. As if trying to start a fire by rubbing two sticks or stones together. I was about to vomit again.

"Shit! Shit! Shit!" she was screaming now, and crying. Suddenly she stopped rubbing and slapped me across the face. Very hard.

I sat up. "What's wrong with you?"

"I love you, I love you! Don't you understand? You've got to care about me!"

She went down again and started to work with her mouth. Then she raised her head. "You've got to fuck me! You've got to! Now! And then you've got to love me!"

"Jennifer, I'm going to be sick."

And I was. Right there. In the bed. And on her. She pulled back and screamed. Screamed. "NOOOOOOO!"

I vomited again, in my lap, and stumbled into the bathroom. When I came out she was in the walk-in closet, in the dark, crying hysterically. I could hear her ripping clothes off hangers. I think she was trying to tear them apart with her hands.

I was awake. It was still dark. This time I did not feel sick. I sat up in the bed. I was remembering how Jennifer had been. The things she had done to me. How desperate she had been. I wanted her.

She was on the other bed. Asleep. Still naked. I lay next to her and kissed her awake. Immediately she pushed me away.

"I'm ready now," I said.

She pushed hard. I fell off the bed.

"Jennifer, wake up! I'm ready. I want you. Feel."

"Get away from me. Don't come near me."

"What's wrong?"

"You're never going to touch me again."

"Yes I am, Jennifer. I'm going to touch you right now." I got back on the bed.

She slapped me. In the face. Even harder than she had before. And this time it was purely anger.

"You bitch!" I grabbed her hand. She lunged at my wrist and bit it. I slapped her with my other hand. She bit harder. I slapped her again, knocking her head away. "You want it that way, baby, that's how you'll have it."

I knelt over her, and she tried to knee me in the balls. She wasn't fooling around. I stopped slapping her and started to punch. Three times I punched her in the face. She fell back on the bed, but when I threw myself on top of her she rolled away, scratching my back. Hurting me. I knew I was bleeding. I knelt up and slapped her again. And again. "You dirty bitch," I was saying. "You dirty, dirty bitch!"

She tried to get out of the bed. I grabbed her by the shoulders and threw her back. I shoved my thigh between her legs and put a hand on her throat to keep her still. She fought anyway, twisting and bucking and scratching, until I started to squeeze her throat.

"Stop," she gasped.

I took my hand away. "I'll stop that," I said, "but I won't stop this."

And I slapped her again and she tried to hit back but I slapped her again, and again, and then forced myself between her legs and into her, deep inside, hurting her. She stopped fighting and started to moan. As soon as she did, I came.

And fell beside her on the bed. Spent and scared. Scared of myself. Scared of whatever had made me that way. Scared of being alive. I fell asleep with my back stinging and my arms still around her. She was trembling and did not say a word.

# Friday

THE FIRST THING I noticed in the morning was that Jennifer was not in the room.

Actually, that was not the first thing. The first thing I noticed was the sun.

A stranger in my room. There had not been bright sun like that since Monday morning. The glare hurt my eyes.

And that is not all that hurt. Again I felt cheated, because marijuana is not supposed to leave a hangover. Then I remembered I had been drinking a little before I smoked.

176

I sat up in the bed, with my head like shattered glass. I could smell vomit, even with the air conditioning on. I got out of bed to look for Jennifer. I couldn't understand why she wasn't in the room. I tried to remember the last time I had seen her. Dinner, yes. I remembered that. And afterward we came up here and everyone was unhappy. She had been making sketches of Blaine. And then . . . the special delivery package, and . . . oh my God. I remembered. Only vaguely, but enough to frighten me.

I hurried toward the living room, the pain in my head even worse. I glanced at the walk-in closet. The door was open and Jennifer's clothes were thrown around the floor. Several of the dresses seemed to have been torn almost in half. There was not one still on a hanger.

I opened the door to the living room. It seemed even brighter than the bedroom. The glare hurt a little too much. I went back to the bathroom and took four aspirin. I was terribly thirsty but I did not need water to drink, I needed Coke.

I opened the door to the living room again.

The brightness was amazing. It was as if we were at the very top of the atmosphere with only a vacuum between us and the sun. A vacuum that sucked in the sun, brilliant and pure.

I squinted and saw Jennifer, motionless on the couch. I walked toward her. She was wearing a red flannel nightshirt that had *Daddy's Little Girl* written across the front in white script. There was a blanket on the floor beside her. The coffee table next to the couch was covered with talcum powder and toiletries and half-empty glasses and beer bottles and several thick, tightly packed marijuana cigarettes.

She woke up as I looked at her and jumped instantly from the couch.

"Oh my God," she said. "What time is it?"

"I don't know."

"My plane!" There was a puffy blue bruise beneath her right eye.

She ran past me toward the bedroom. I turned and followed. She picked up the portable alarm clock that she had kept by the side of her bed. "Thank God," she said. "It's only quarter to nine." Then she walked past me the other way, back to the couch. She lay down, and pulled the blanket over her head.

"Jennifer?"

"Yes?" she said from beneath the blanket.

"What plane?"

She folded the blanket down to her chin. "My plane to San Francisco."

"That doesn't leave until Sunday. This is Friday."

She smiled. "There's been a change in plans."

"What do you mean?"

"I'm leaving today. National at two P.M."

"What?"

"I'm going home."

"No you're not. You can't."

"It is ironic, though."

"What's ironic?"

"That the day I'm leaving is the first good day of sun. I wanted so much to get a real tan."

"Jennifer, this is crazy. You're not leaving. We've got two more days."

"Ssssh. Just hold me and talk to me for as much time as we have left."

"Ssssh, my ass. What is this about leaving? Because of last night?"

"Sit down," she said.

I sat next to her on the couch.

"I am leaving today," she said, very slowly, reaching up to stroke my face as she spoke, "not because of last night, but because I cannot stay with you any longer after what I have found out."

"What have you found out?"

She looked at me as maternally as she could with blood-shot eyes. "That you are dishonoring your wife."

"What?"

"That you are dishonoring your wife and that I would be dishonoring myself if I were to allow it to continue."

"Jennifer, what are you talking about?"

"I told you all this last night but I guess you don't remember."

"I guess I don't."

"Remember yesterday morning when you told me not to answer the phone?"

"When I told you what?"

"When you were going out to get a paper and you told me to be sure not to answer the phone."

"Oh, yes. Of course."

"Well, that was the beginning. Do you have any idea what an insult that was?"

"Jennifer, that wasn't any insult. That was common sense."

"It was an insult. It made me feel cheap. Like some whore you had shipped in for the week that you didn't want anyone to know about."

"Jennifer, that's ridiculous."

"Wait. Then I started to think: why doesn't he want me to answer the phone? That's why I called Patsy. To see if she thought it was as bad as I did. I don't always trust my own reactions."

"And did she?"

"Worse. She told me to come home yesterday."

"Jennifer, this is absurd. I didn't mean anything by that. It was just an obvious matter of tactics."

"There! Tactics! That's it!"

"What's it?"

"Tactics. Why can't I answer your phone? If I can sleep with you."

"You know perfectly well. Because suppose it was my wife calling. Who are you supposed to be? The chambermaid?"

"See. That's what I didn't understand. Until yesterday."

"What didn't you understand?"

"I didn't understand that your wife didn't know."

"What?"

"I knew you were married—I knew it from the interview—but when you went ahead and asked me to come, I assumed it was all right. That you were married and had children and stayed married for their sake and you had worked out an arrangement with your wife."

"I don't understand this."

"It never occurred to me that she didn't know I was coming here this week."

"How the hell could it have occurred to you that she would?"

"I assumed you had told her."

"Jennifer!"

"Yes. Now I understand. Now I understand it's a big sneak. You're dishonoring your wife. And that's why I'm leaving. If I had thought for a minute that she didn't know about this, I wouldn't have come. It just never occurred to me that you were that type."

"What type?"

"The type who would dishonor his wife."

"Jennifer, you're being ridiculous. What am I supposed to say? 'Honey, I'm, ah, going to spend a week in Florida with a girl I met this morning in San Francisco'?"

"You have to."

"What?"

"It's the only honorable way."

"Jennifer, I've never seen this kind of naïveté."

"You think it's naïve to believe in honor?"

"I know it's naïve to think I would have told my wife."

"Well, I suspected yesterday when you said I couldn't answer the phone, but when Barnaby told me for sure last night, I called the airlines right away."

"This is crazy. This is too crazy to believe. I don't know where to start. But wait: what made Barnaby tell you anything?"

"I was starting to call her."

"Who?"

"Your wife."

"What?"

"I was going to call her and tell her that I loved you and that you would be seeing a lot of me in the future and that I hoped we could all be friends because I had so much respect for her as the mother of your children."

"Jesus Christ."

"That's what Barnaby said. Then he told me he was sure she didn't know you were down here with me. I was stunned. That you had made me a part of something so dishonorable." She smiled at me. Sweetly. "So—I owe it to your wife, as one woman to another—as one human being to another—not to stay another day."

"Jennifer."

"I owe it to myself, too. I have too much respect for myself. I hope never to be dishonored in that way. So I've really got no choice."

"Jennifer, this—"

"The only way I would stay is if you promised me you'd leave your wife."

"What?"

"I think you should leave her anyway. If you don't love her, you have to leave her."

"Jennifer, I—"

"If you don't love a person, it's a dishonor to live with them. And you couldn't love her or you wouldn't have brought me here."

"Stop."

"You must give her a chance to build a new life. With someone who does love her. While she's still young enough."

"Jennifer, I think we're getting very far off the subject. I think also that you are giving out a lot of strong advice based on very limited information."

"I don't need information. All I need to know is right and wrong."

"I don't want marital advice from you. I only want you to stay here for the rest of the week."

"No."

"Why not?"

"You're dishonoring your wife."

"Jennifer, what does that mean? That's not even a word."

"It's a concept. I know what it means. And you do, too. I only hope my husband will never dishonor me in that way. In fact, I know he never will, because the man I'll marry will be too good—too much of a man—to act this way. I thought you were that good. I was wrong. So I have to leave."

The phone rang. It was Blaine. No *Telegraphs* at five A.M. again. He was going downtown and wanted me to go with him. He was in the lobby, ready. It was nine-twenty and cold outside. I said I'd be down in ten minutes.

"Jennifer, I've got to go out with Barnaby for papers. We're going to get three. One for you. I'll be back in fifteen minutes. You can't leave today. That's all there is to it."

Why did I want her to stay? After all the craziness and violence of the night before? After she had so convincingly substantiated the worst of Blaine's opinions?

I wasn't sure. But I thought it had something to do with

the fact that once she left, there would be no one around me to tell me how splendid I was. How famous and important. No one to flatter me, and act thrilled by just being at my side.

And, I reflected, it might be quite a while before any-one would act that way again. Maybe never.

I would go home Sunday, to my wife, who was so full of grudges and demands. All of them justified, but not any less burdensome for that. And home to a future that offered no guarantee of success.

The four months of stardom were ending. Which made the two days that remained seem so crucial. And made Jennifer, quite simply, seem essential.

She stood up and smiled.

"Suppose you were my coach," she said.

"What?"

"Suppose you were my coach. In a sport. Or my guid-ance counselor. Or a teacher who had established a close personal relationship with me. And I came to you in this situation and asked your advice. And you would make your decision based strictly on what was best for me. What would you tell me to do?"

"Jennifer, I'm not your . . . coach. I'm—"

"Come on. You're trying to decide the best thing for me. For Jennifer. For my future. What would it be?"

"I don't know. How can I answer that?"

"You already have. See, you know it, too. There are forty-eight hours left in this week, and if I stayed here, it would just be selfish and dishonorable. And I'd be wasting those forty-eight hours. I've told you how precious I think time is, and how I think the greatest sin man can commit is to waste it. I can't commit that sin. I have too much respect for myself."

"Jennifer, I'm going to put on pants and shoes and go out with Barnaby. I'll be back in twenty minutes. You can't leave."

"I'll be packing while you're gone."

I met Blaine in the lobby.

"Thanks a lot."

He smiled. "What for?"

"I leave you alone with my girl for an hour and the next thing I know she's going home."

"Hey, buddy, you'd better thank me for that. Seriously. That's the biggest favor I've ever done anyone. And you have no idea how hard it was."

"How hard what was?"

"Talking her into leaving. She would have none of it. Crying, ripping off her clothes, saying no, no, she'd rather kill herself first."

"What are you talking about?"

"You went inside to answer the phone, right? And remember? She was already crying in my arms?"

"Yes."

"Well, she calms down a little and goes to sit by herself on the couch and then she lights up another of her surprises from back home. I'm half asleep, really zonked out on that stuff, and the next thing I hear is her asking an information operator for your phone number. That woke me up in a hurry. I grabbed the phone away from her and then we went through a whole hysterical scene—"

"About how I was dishonoring my wife?"

"Exactly. Whatever that means. Anyway, she screamed a lot of crap about how we were 'dishonoring' her, too, and then she started throwing punches at me, saying I was a part of it, I was just as bad as you. You wouldn't have believed it. I had to sit on her for five minutes. On the floor.

"Finally, I get her nice and calm again and explain to her that this is getting to be too much of a strain for her emotionally and that she'd better go home. I thought she was agreeing with me, so I call National Airlines—"

"Wait a minute. You called the airline?"

"Yes."

"She told me she did."

"She was still sitting on the floor. As soon as I make the reservation she starts crying and screaming again, and that's when she started tearing off her clothes. And all this crap about how she can't go home until you say you love her, and she'll kill herself first. Right about then I was believing her. I sat with her another half-hour, calming her down, and finally she said she wanted to go to bed with you, so I left. But thank God she's going home. That's the first lucky thing that's happened to us since we got here. That broad really scares me. She goes out a window and they find all that dope in your room and you've lost more than a few horse races, pal."

"Oh, hell," I said.

186

"What?"
"I was just trying to talk her into staying."

Well, that was that. Blaine was right, of course. Besides, he said he needed uninterrupted concentration these last two days. For our comeback.

At least I could pretend to be noble. I would go back to the room and walk up to Jennifer and put my arm around her—just like a coach—and say, "You're right, you know. And I'm proud of you for making this decision."

That would be nice. She would go home respecting me and I could concentrate on the horses with Blaine.

We drove to the newsstand at Second and Flagler. The papers were in. He bought two, not three. The morning was cold. But clear, blue, and soaked with sun. Not Florida sun, but the sun that shines on New England in October. It was as if the past three days of grayness and rain had been a slide on a projector and someone had pushed the button overnight. I was filled suddenly with the rhythm and flavor of autumn.

I was whistling as I walked into the room. Jennifer was not on the couch. I walked into the bedroom. She was lying on my bed, facing away from me, toward the window. Under a sheet. Her red nightshirt was on the floor beside her.

"Hey, you packed already?"
She turned over and smiled. Such a warm smile.
I tossed my *Telegraph* on the dresser.
"Where's mine?" she said.

I laughed. "What are you going to do, figure out the races on the plane?"

"No, silly." She was grinning. She sat up in the bed, the sheet falling to her waist. She was naked. The nipples on her breasts looked very large.

"Guess what?" she said, in the tone women use to announce that they are pregnant.

"What?"

"I'm staying."

There is no sense going into too much detail about what happened next. It started with me saying, "Guess what," and her saying, "What?" and me saying, "No you're not," and it went on from there.

Finally I went into the bathroom and locked the door behind me and got into the shower and turned it on as hot as I could stand it and stayed there for half an hour. The pounding on the door did not last nearly as long as it might have, all things considered.

When I came out of the shower she was gone. So was the $20 I had thrown at her for cab fare. Her bags were still there, though. Unpacked.

Blaine came knocking at my door, saying let's go, let's go, our great comeback is about to start.

"Jennifer has disappeared."

"Well, hallelujah."

"No, Barnaby. I'm worried."

"What for? She's still got three hours to make her plane."

"I don't think we should just leave her like this. I mean, without even saying goodbye."

"Look. I'm going to the track. You're so worried about her, you can go to San Francisco."

Finally he agreed to wait half an hour while I looked for her. Through the giant, empty lobbies, out back by the bay and the pools. Up and down the sidewalk in front of the hotel. Palm trees blew in the breeze, with bright blue and bright sun all around them. I could not believe how clean the day was: like an incision.

I did not find Jennifer. I came back and checked the room. She had not returned. The bags were still there. She had left no messages at the desk. It was twelve-fifteen. Blaine was in the lobby.

"Time to go racing, buddy. We've got a bet in the first one today."

"I'd really like to find her, Barnaby."

"I'd really like to win a bet."

So we left. With the top down and our collars turned up against the cool. And me looking behind us until we got to the expressway.

Pumpkins would have seemed more fitting for the infield than flamingos. There was that much clean autumn in the air. I sat on the grass behind the clubhouse and turned my face toward the sun, seeing new brilliance in the colors and shapes I had been looking at every day. Out of the sun it was chilly, and Blaine, complaining of it, had gone to an indoor restaurant for soup.

It was New England, not Florida. Jennifer, for the first time, would have felt something of the east.

Our comeback did not last long. We bet favorites in each of the first three races and lost them all.

"That's it," Blaine said evenly. "That's our last bet of the day."

"Already?"

He nodded.

"But tomorrow's our last day."

"I know. Maybe we'll have a big day tomorrow."

"But what do we do the rest of today?"

He shrugged. "I'm going to sit here and watch the races."

"But not bet?"

"There's nothing to bet on. There's nothing else that qualifies all day."

"Then let's get out of here. Let's not stay here."

He shook his head. "Sorry," he said. "We have no place to go."

I left him and went back outside to sit on the grass. He stayed in his seat, coat collar turned up, hands in pockets, staring at the four hundred flamingos that flew aimlessly around their island, trying to keep warm.

I bet two more races without telling him. Trying to handicap them from the *Telegraph* myself. I lost them both.

Blaine stayed in his seat for four hours, until the tenth race had been run. Sticking to his principles like an old woman clinging to the roof of her house in a flood.

At the hotel, Blaine insisted that he go to my room with me, in case I was about to find Jennifer's body on the bathroom floor. Or an open window with curtains flapping. Or maybe just Jennifer—grinning, kissing me, asking us how we had done.

Instead, there was only a note:

Dear Boys:

How could you break up the act without even saying goodbye. Hard to imagine you could turn against me that fast. Oh, well. I'm not the type to carry a grudge. I'm taking my plane, as instructed. Hope the taxi driver will not mind tears. It was real, I loved you both. In different ways of course. If you get to Salt Lake City, don't hesitate to call. If I can ever help you in any way, please let me know. (That goes for <u>both</u> of you.) Wish me luck with The Dream Team. You'll probably be reading my by-line someday soon and both of you can say, "We knew her when . . ."

I went into the bedroom. On a dresser there, Jennifer had left the sketches she had made of Blaine—not very good, really—and the peace-symbol wristwatch. Next to them was an envelope, sealed, with *For Your Eyes Only* printed across the front.

I opened it and took out a piece of paper. It contained some lines from Wordsworth. I guess it was something she had memorized.

> What though the radiance which was once so bright
> Be now for ever taken from my sight,

Though nothing can bring back the hour
Of splendor in the grass, of glory in the flower;
    We will grieve not, rather find
    Strength in what remains behind;
    In the primal sympathy
    Which having been must ever be;
    In the soothing thoughts that spring
    Out of human suffering;
    In the faith that looks through death,
In years that bring the philosophic mind.

"Jesus Christ," I said out loud, and crumpled up the paper and threw it in a wastebasket and went up to Blaine's room to drink Scotch.

I found him on his hands and knees on the floor, folding the *Morning Telegraph*s and stacking them neatly into piles.

"Where's your Scotch?"

"On the bar," he said, not looking up.

I walked past him and noticed he was sweating despite how cool the day was and the air conditioning, which operated despite the weather, in the room.

The top of the bar had been cleared. The slide rules, adding machine, loose-leaf binders filled with graphs—all of these had been put somewhere out of sight. I put some ice cubes in a glass and poured some Scotch.

"Well," I said. "She's gone."

Blaine did not answer.

"Barnaby. Tomorrow's our last day. I've lost eighteen hundred dollars. What are we going to do?"

He was at the other end of the room, folding up his last row of papers. He did not answer until he had finished. Then he stood. Still at the other end of the room. When he spoke, it was so softly that I did not think I had heard him correctly.

"What? What did you say?"

He repeated it. A little louder. "I'm going home."

"When? You can't. We've got racing tomorrow."

"I'm going home," he said again. "Tonight. At nine o'clock."

"But, Barnaby, what about tomorrow?"

This made him laugh. To himself, not to me. "What about tomorrow, he wants to know." He laughed again. "What I want to know is what about the rest of my life."

"Barnaby, wait a minute, you can't be serious. Tomorrow's our last chance to get even."

"What are you talking about, kid?"

"The race track. Tomorrow's Saturday. Our last day."

"There's no getting even, kid. There's no getting even at the end of a week like this."

"But we're so due. If we just hit a couple at decent prices. Or maybe we can play a few Daily Doubles. Look, I'm almost busted but I'll wire for more dough tonight. I'll get it in time. We can be back out there by noon and take one more shot."

He was smiling at me. Not without affection, I thought, but with more sadness than anything else. "You've got a long way to go, kid. You've barely started."

"What do you mean? Barely started what?"

"I've based my entire life on a particular, very specific,

193

assumption. Namely: that a human being of normal intelligence, who is willing to apply diligent effort and impose rigorous self-discipline on his impulses, can, over a protracted period of time, earn a substantial profit by wagering on the outcome of horse races. It was my dream, kid. The dream I lived my life by."

He stared over my shoulder, out the window, at the shimmering bay. "This week I've come to realize that the assumption, quite probably, is false."

He turned, and bent down, and started to lift the stacks of *Telegraphs* off the floor.

"But all those years. Twenty-five years. You've been winning."

"No."

"What?"

He was not smiling any more. "I haven't been winning."

"You mean—"

"I've been trying, kid. Trying for twenty-five years. And coming close. Close enough to keep me going. Winning for a few weeks or a few months at a time and thinking, finally, I've beaten you, you bastards, and then going sour. Going back to my study and dragging up all the fundamentals again. The last couple of years, kid, I really thought I had it. No shit. I've really done very well on the coast. That's why I decided to come back."

"To Hialeah?"

"To Hialeah. This was the track that broke me in '58. This was the track that made me go west. Go west? Christ, Hialeah made me cut my hair and shave my mustache and change my name. I left a few people behind, kid. A few people I owed money to."

He walked across the room, to the bar, and poured himself more Scotch. His perspiration, I noticed, had dried up.

"For twelve years out there, I really thought I was putting it together. Finally. After I'd seen it ruin my life several times. I finally thought, this year, that I was ready to come back. This was where I would prove it, kid. This was the track I had to beat." He drank deeply from his glass. "I was going to pay them back. With the money I won I was going to pay back everybody I could find who was still alive. I was going to put ads in the papers. With my real name. Saying I'd beaten Hialeah and now I could pay off my debts."

He drained the glass and laid it gently on the bar. "You know why I wanted you to come? The two of you? You know why I was so agreeable when you got your crazy idea? I was scared to come back alone."

"Scared of the people you owed money to?"

"No. I wasn't scared of the people. What I was scared of was the track."

He came around the bar and shook my hand again. "So long, kid. I've got to call a bellboy for the bags."

"How did you get packed so fast?"

"I packed this morning. I knew it was going to happen like this. And that's why I wanted to stay this afternoon, even after I'd stopped betting. Because I knew I'd never be back."

"Jesus, Barnaby—"

"I'm sorry, kid. I am truly, truly sorry I got you involved. And I'm sorry about the money that it's cost you. I had thought—if he believes I can do it, and he's with me out there every day, then maybe I'll keep believing it myself. Confidence is very important with the horses, kid. And that's what I was trying to drum up."

"But—"

"I got to go. Be careful, kid. Be careful of these bastards. They can hurt you."

He was halfway to the telephone when he stopped. "Oh. I almost forgot." He laughed. "You think you could loan me ten bucks for the cab?"

I went downstairs and ordered a grilled-cheese sandwich and a bottle of milk for my dinner. I watched the sun set on the bay as I ate. The room was very quiet without Jennifer. She had been crazy, but all things considered, I think I liked her.

# Saturday

AS SOON AS I woke up I called my publisher. I told him I needed $2,000 before noon. He said it would be difficult on a Saturday.

"Please. I'm desperate."

"What the hell's been going on down there? This is four thousand dollars in a week."

"Please. Just send the money."

There were clouds in the sky again, but no rain. I wondered if it was warm or cool. I had to call the weather bureau to find out. All the windows in the hotel were hermetically sealed to hold the air conditioning in.

The weather bureau said the temperature was eighty-six degrees. Partly cloudy, chance of showers overnight. I took a shower by myself and kept the hot water on all the way. Then I got dressed and walked downtown to buy a *Telegraph.*

JOIE DE VIVRE, SEA CHANGE CLASH IN FLAMINGO. There would also be eight other horses in the race. The purse was $117,000. Joie de Vivre and Sea Change had both had workouts over the Hialeah track Friday morning. Both trainers said they were satisfied with the results. Then I saw the smaller head in the middle of the page. "Rand Ill," it said. "May Miss Flamingo."

John Rand had the flu. He had been forced to cancel all his mounts yesterday and was reported to have a fever of 103°. I had been so dazed I had not noticed he didn't ride on Friday. There was some chance he would recover for the Flamingo, the story said, but his physician did not think it likely. The trainer of Joie de Vivre said he did not know who could ride the horse if Rand could not.

When I got back to the hotel, there was a phone call from my publisher. He said the money had been arranged. I could pick it up at the Western Union office, in Miami.

I walked back downtown, a mile and a half. I felt like walking. I kept the *Telegraph* folded neatly under my arm. I had not even opened it to look at the past performance charts.

I had to wait until twelve-thirty for the money. I sat on a bench in the drab, stuffy office and tried not to think about what I knew I was going to do. The Western Union office in Miami was bigger than the one in Fort Lauderdale had been eight years before, but otherwise it looked pretty much the same. I listened to the clicking of the machines and hoped for the rapid recovery of John Rand. Two different Negroes came in barefoot, reeking of cheap wine, and said they were expecting $100 from their cousins in Chicago. Neither got it.

I had to sign a lot of papers to get my money. The man behind the counter was short and bald and wore rimless glasses and obviously did not approve of this much money being transferred through his office. I think that he also did not approve of someone as young as myself being able to say there would be $2,000 coming from New York and then having it turn out to be true. Years of saying no to Negroes with cousins in Chicago had given him a distaste for saying yes.

I rode in an air-conditioned cab to the track. The driver told me to close my windows. I said I liked the warm air. He said goddamnit he had paid $450 to get his cab air-conditioned and he was goddamn well going to use it. I told him I was going to be sick to my stomach any minute and if the windows were rolled up I might have to throw up all over the back seat of his cab. He drove seventy miles an hour on the expressway, with the windows down. He was very happy to be rid of me at the track.

It was crowded. The first big crowd of the week. Saturdays, of course, are always crowded, but this was Flamingo Day and it brought the biggest crowd of the year.

I was too late to get a good seat. I climbed to a far corner of the clubhouse and managed to find an unreserved seat next to two used-car dealers from the Bronx who said they had flown down just for the race. They immediately started to tell me about how they never paid any tolls when they drove over the bridges of New York. They used the exact-change lanes all the time and just drove straight through. Neither of them had paid a nickel for two years and neither of them ever had been caught. "Do you know how much that adds up to over a year?" one kept saying. "Compounded, compounded," the other one said. They were drinking beer from paper cups and eating peanuts. They said if I was ever in the Bronx and needed a car, I should see them. I tore the back page from my *Morning Telegraph* and folded it between the wooden slats of my seat to reserve it. I said I would be back before the big race. "Sea Change," they said. "Sea Change is a winner."

I walked out back and sat on the grass amid old men with pale thin arms and short-sleeved shirts. I wondered what it would be like to have flesh that hung so slackly from your bones. There were high, hazy clouds in the sky, but nothing ominous. I looked in my program at the listings for the Flamingo. There was hope: Rand was listed as the rider.

But then the track announcer, the little man with the voice like a bird, announced the program changes for the day. Mostly these were overweights—jockeys who could not sweat off the final pound or two to get down to the weight their horses were supposed to carry. So the horse would carry more weight than he had been assigned. It was not easy being a jockey. Getting yelled at by a trainer because you weighed 114 pounds instead of 112. And having to make yourself throw up whenever you were undisciplined enough to eat potatoes.

The announcer was reading off changes in riders. For the second, fourth, and fifth races. Changes on horses John Rand had been scheduled to ride. The announcer got to the eighth race—"the twen-ty-third running of the Fla-*ming*-go Stakes. For three-year-olds, at one mile and an eighth. For number three," he said, "Jwah de Veev-ruh, the jockey will be—Sonny Holiday."

A murmur ran through the crowd. Holiday riding the favorite in the Flamingo!

It was unusual, very unusual, no matter how hot an apprentice jockey was, to put him on a good horse in a race as important as this. For one thing, in a stakes race, his five-pound weight allowance was not granted. He had to ride on equal terms with other jockeys. For another, with $117,000 in the pot, the riders would be trying particularly hard. No helpful gestures would be extended toward a kid who was riding his first big race. Holiday's inexperience could only work against him. For him to get the mount on Joie de Vivre anyway meant the trainer had an incredible amount of confidence in his ability. A dozen veterans, including some of the leading riders at the meeting, did not have mounts in this race. Any of them could have been engaged to replace Rand. Instead it was Holiday. And this despite the miserable streak he had endured Friday. I had been suffering too much myself to notice at the time, but Holiday had ridden in all ten races Friday, four times on favorites, and had not once even finished in the money. This meant that in his past nineteen rides, he had won only once. Winning the Flamingo on Joie de Vivre would be a pretty convincing way to end the slump.

I wandered around the track all afternoon. Not even tempted to bet the early races. I looked at the birds and the fish, and I drank false-bottomed beer at the Sidewalk Café. Despite everything, I thought back with longing to the first day we had spent there. The three of us, seeming so bright and fresh and full of hope.

I stood by the walking ring for several races, watching Holiday climb on his mounts. Always it was the same: the cold eyes looking somewhere else; the expressionless face; the hands slowly, almost unconsciously, twisting the reins.

The crowd at the walking ring was large. A lot of people yelled encouragement to Holiday. He was their darling despite the recent slump: he had blond hair and he was still on top of the standings. He never looked at them, of course; only his hands moved, and they communicated only with his horse.

Holiday rode five times in the first seven races, and managed only a third. Even that was on a 4–5 favorite that had won five races in a row. This meant Holiday would go into the Flamingo with only one win in his past twenty-four races.

I kept drinking beer to keep me calm. And I wandered in the sunlight, trying not to think. I spoke to no one. Except for the used-car men, no one had tried to speak to me. The sun moved slowly across the sky, the pale haze grew thicker, and with it came a glare. As soon as the result of the seventh race was official, I went to the $100 window on the first floor of the clubhouse.

There was no one else there. I would be the first person to make a $100 bet on the Flamingo.

"Number three," I said. "Five times."

My Western Union money had been given to me in $100 bills. Twenty of them. I slid five across the counter toward the seller.

He looked at me with curiosity. This was downstairs, and I had been betting upstairs all week. He punched the tickets. The machine made a low, whirring sound, and they popped up through the metal slot, one after the other. I scooped them off the counter with my hand.

Then I went to the men's room. The nervousness was rushing over me; I was starting to tremble, and almost half an hour still remained before the race.

I came out of the men's room and went back to the $100 window. This time there were two people ahead of me in line. I heard the man before me say, "Number Seven." That was Sea Change. But the man had only bet him once.

"Number three," I said. "Five times."

The seller exhaled slowly through his mouth. He looked at me evenly, wondering what I knew. The machine whirred, the tickets popped up, and I put them in the breast pocket of my shirt with the others. Then I went outside to the walking ring to get myself a good position by the fence.

There was an odds board I could see from the walking

ring. Joie de Vivre was at even money in the early betting. Sea Change was 7–5. Nothing else in the race was less than 6–1.

There were big crowds by the paddock where the horses were being saddled. The biggest, I noticed, was in front of stall number 7. The second largest was in front of number 3. I waited at the walking ring to which the horses would be led. The crowd around me began to grow. By the time the horses started over, they were eight deep behind me and pushing forward. I was squeezed against the fence and sweating in the afternoon haze.

I recognized Joie de Vivre right away. He walked tall, with his head held high, the way a thoroughbred horse was supposed to. A Negro groom led him by a halter, walking slowly, as the guards cleared a path through the crowd.

His ears were twitching and there was a light film of sweat on his coat. It could have been just the heat, or it could have been a touch of nervousness because of the crowd. Or maybe because of the race. He couldn't know he'd be running against Sea Change today, but he might have picked up some of the tension of his handlers.

The ten horses were led slowly around the walking ring in single file. There was a black colt, very skittish, behind Joie de Vivre in the line. He kept twisting his head from side to side, and once or twice he tried to rear up on his hind legs. His eyes looked wild and frightened and there was thick white kidney sweat between his legs. I looked at the odds board and saw that he was 40–1. The odds on Joie de Vivre and Sea Change had not changed.

Sonny Holiday, as usual, was the first jockey into the ring. And, as usual, there was no expression on his face. He might have been about to ride in a $5,000 claiming race instead of the Flamingo Stakes.

The race could make a big difference to his career. Besides the $7,000 he would get as his ten percent share of the winner's purse—if he won—there would be the publicity. Holiday would not ride Joie de Vivre again, once Rand recovered, but trainers all over the country would know that he had ridden the winner in the Flamingo, at equal weights with older jockeys. It would be a big help on the day when he left his apprentice status behind.

Holiday nodded, staring at the ground, as Joie de Vivre's trainer spoke. The walking of the horses had stopped now, and each was standing still, waiting to be mounted. Joie de Vivre stood calmly, his ears still twitching slightly. A good sign, I thought, a sign that he was alert.

Sea Change stood on the other side of the ring. He was the only horse in the field bigger than Joie de Vivre, and the only other one to which people in the crowd around the circle were pointing. I held my binoculars up to him and saw he was chewing lightly on his bit.

"Riders up!"

The trainer patted Holiday lightly on the shoulder. One of Joie de Vivre's owners held out a hand. Holiday ignored it. He hopped lightly into the saddle and began to twirl the reins around his hand.

The horses walked once around the ring. The crowd

outside pushed forward, straining for a look, until I thought the fence might bend. People were leaning against me from all sides, talking to each other or talking to themselves. The odds board showed no changes: Joie de Vivre at even money; Sea Change at 7–5.

Holiday sat straight up in the saddle, the reins held in one hand, his other lightly caressing Joie de Vivre's neck. If the horse knew it was not Rand on his back, he gave no sign. He walked with an even stride, his head still high, his eyes taking in the milling and shouldering that was going on outside the fence. The black colt behind him balked and started to prance sideways in the ring. Joie de Vivre continued slowly along his path. Sea Change stood calmly, looking almost lordly, as he waited for the black colt to move again.

Then I heard the bugle blow, and the horses walked toward the track. The crowd broke up like rush hour on the subway, everyone suddenly making up his mind who to bet, and suddenly afraid that the sellers would run out of tickets.

I walked quickly to the escalator and rode to the third floor, where I hoped my seat had not been taken. I stopped at the men's room on the way. When I came out of the men's room, instead of turning right, to my seat, I turned left, toward the $100 window.

"Number three," I said. "Five times."

This was the seller who had been giving me tickets all week. All losers, except for the place ticket on Sad State.

He recognized me and smiled as he punched out the tickets. "Good luck," he said.

"Thanks."

I turned away and walked along the crowded cement aisle. I paused behind a crowd at an intersection and trained my binoculars on the track. Joie de Vivre was galloping freely in the warm-up. Holiday was standing high in the saddle, keeping his rein taut. Joie de Vivre was a little darker than Chateaugay had been, but from a distance, through binoculars, he looked almost the same.

Instead of going to my seat, I turned and ran back to the window. There were only two minutes now before the race. The horses had stopped galloping, had turned, and were walking slowly toward the starting gate in the haze. Behind them, the flamingos were clustered on the island, the Indian standing up in his canoe. Everyone was ready for the race.

"Number three," I said. "Five times."

My mouth was dry. My voice small. This time the seller did not smile. I took the tickets and pushed through the crowd to my seat. I got there just in time to check the odds board as the horses were led into the gate. Joie de Vivre had dropped to 4–5.

The Hialeah track was exactly a mile and an eighth in diameter. This meant the horses would start at the finish line and run one full lap around the track. There was not much of a straightaway before the first turn, but with the whole backstretch to run, and then the homestretch, position on the first turn did not seem of crucial importance. None of these horses had ever run a mile and an eighth before. All were carrying 126 pounds, a lot of weight for a three-year-old colt. It was the same weight they would be required to carry a mile and a quarter if they made the Kentucky Derby. Joie de Vivre would make it. That much I was sure of.

And I would make it, too.

"It is now post time," the announcer said, and almost immediately they were off.

Joie de Vivre sprang first from the gate. With Holiday urging him, he quickly moved ahead of the two horses who had started inside him, and Holiday pulled him in to the rail. At a mile and an eighth he wanted to save all the ground he could.

Sea Change had not been so fortunate on the break. Getting out of the gate more slowly, he had little choice but to move to the inside, behind the pack, as they pounded toward the turn. Joie de Vivre was fourth on the rail, with Sea Change running next to last.

I was not worried about the horses who were leading now. When the time came, I was certain Joie de Vivre could pass them. There was some danger, of course, that Holiday would get boxed in and be unable to move, but after having watched him for a week, I was sure he was clever enough to avoid that.

He kept Joie de Vivre along the rail as they came out of the turn into the backstretch. Sea Change, from far back, came off the rail to make a move. I watched him swing four wide and charge down the middle of the track. His jockey wanted him much closer to the front when they hit the final turn. Holiday was keeping tight rein on Joie de Vivre. There were two horses about two lengths ahead of him, and one about a half-length ahead alongside. Sea Change, however, was still moving, and drawing close.

When Chateaugay had won his Derby, I had been unable to see the race. At Churchill Downs, without a box seat, it is difficult even to see a horse on Derby Day. I had climbed a camera tower, but without binoculars, all I could see was the pack—moving slowly, it seemed, around the crowd that had massed in the infield. I did not realize Chateaugay had won until the race was over and he galloped toward where I was standing, far past the finish line, with all the other horses trailing behind.

But now I was able to watch every stride that Joie de Vivre took.

Going into the final turn, Sea Change, still on the outside, moved past Joie de Vivre toward the leaders. His jockey wanted to take no chance of moving inside, behind tired horses, and maybe getting trapped.

That was what Holiday had been waiting for. He had wanted Sea Change to move first. As soon as Sea Change passed him, Holiday pulled Joie de Vivre off the rail. He ran right at Sea Change's heels, and the two of them surged to the lead at the top of the homestretch. Even through my tension now, I could hear the screaming of the crowd. The used-car dealers were drunk, and didn't have binoculars, and kept yelling "Who's ahead?"

It was Sea Change by a length and a half as they started down the final three-sixteenths of a mile. Sea Change never had been passed in the homestretch, but Joie de Vivre never had failed to pass.

The process by which Joie de Vivre overtook Sea Change in the homestretch seemed very slow. The whole race, in fact, seemed to have slipped into a dimension in which time did not exist. Actually, everything happened very fast. Eighteen seconds, perhaps, for the last three-sixteenths of a mile, and the end of Joie de Vivre's career.

By the eighth pole they were even, and by the sixteenth pole, Joie de Vivre had forged ahead. By a nose, then a head, then a neck. Holiday was whipping furiously, although Joie de Vivre had never been whipped before.

It was perhaps 100 yards from the finish that it happened. Joie de Vivre had pulled a full length ahead. I did not actually see his foot hit the ground, because I was concentrating on Holiday and his whip. But I saw the horse bobble—then lurch—as if he had stepped in a hole.

I knew it was bad because I knew there were no holes in the track. He was a full length ahead and less than a dozen strides from the finish, but I knew he had broken his ankle.

I had never seen a horse break an ankle before, so I'm not sure how I knew. But something about the sudden lurch—his foot hitting the hard surface wrong, hitting wrong because he was striding unevenly now from fatigue. And then the full weight of his thousand-pound body coming down on top of the bad step.

I expected him to fall. But he didn't fall. And Holiday, instead of pulling him up, to stop him from hurting himself any more, kept him running. Incredibly, Holiday never even relented with the whip.

"Pull him up!" I shouted. "Pull him up!" I did not care about my money. I didn't even think about the money. All I could think of was the horse.

Joie de Vivre's nose weaved back and forth like the front end of a speedboat, and with every stride, his distress grew clearly worse. Sea Change, tired but not quitting, ranged up again outside him. They were within a head of each other and then within a nose. And Joie de Vivre splintering more bone with every stride.

It was a photograph at the finish. I could not tell who had won.

About fifty yards past the finish line, as Holiday tried to pull him up, Joie de Vivre suddenly went down. As if the track had been pulled out from beneath him. Holiday rolled clear and jumped to his feet, unhurt. Joie de Vivre lay writhing on the ground. The other horses, who had finished far back in the race, galloped past.

It took almost five minutes for the judges to decide, from the photograph, that Joie de Vivre had won the race. When his number went up, there was a great cheer from the crowd.

I did not even see it get posted. My binoculars had never left the horse. I saw Holiday walk away, out of my range of vision, without looking back. And then I saw nothing but the horse, twisting in agony in the dirt, trying time after time to get up, but never able to.

The van got to him quickly, and after a ten-minute struggle they were able to get him inside. The doors closed behind him and the van pulled away down the track. Away from the winner's circle, toward the barns.

I pushed my way past the used-car men, and rode down the escalator in a daze. I knew it was bad. I knew it was very bad for the horse. I walked through the crowd on the ground floor, through the green-tiled lobby, past the barber shop and souvenir stand, to the pink stucco gate that led outside. My only thought was to get away from the track as fast as I could.

Then I remembered.

I had $2,000 in winning tickets in my pocket.

I turned, still dazed, and went to the $100 cashier. There was a small line. Ahead of me and behind me people in the line wore happy grins.

I collected $3,800 at the window. The cashier asked if I wanted a check. I shook my head and put the cash in my pocket without counting it. Then I walked out of the track and got a cab.


I packed quickly and went to the airport. I had no reservation but I was sure I'd get a plane. As it turned out, I had to wait an hour and a half, but I got on an eight o'clock flight. I said a coach seat would be fine, but all they had left was first class.

Then I called my wife and told her I'd be home. She said she would meet me at the airport.

I went to the newsstand. A new edition of the Sunday *Herald* had just come in. I turned immediately to the sports page. The first thing I saw was the picture. Then I let my eyes read the headline.

Joie de Vivre Destroyed After Triumph in Flamingo

The subhead said: "Shatters Foreleg in Beating Sea Change by Nose"

On the other side of the page there was a picture of Sonny Holiday shaking hands with the Governor of

Florida after the race. He was smiling for the first time all week.

I drank the two martinis the stewardess gave me and asked her for a third.

"We're not supposed to," she said, smiling coyly. She was blond and tan and looked like a thousand other stewardesses.

"Please," I said. "I really need it."

Then she saw the *Telegraph* in my lap. I had been planning to read again, in numbers and abbreviations, the story of Joie de Vivre's career. The characters in a play, Blaine had said. All we have to figure out is the plot.

"Ooh," said the stewardess, sounding not unlike Jennifer. "Have you been to the horse races?"

I nodded.

"Ooh, I love the horse races. Which track is open now, Gulfstream Park?"

"Hialeah."

"Oh, that's the most beautiful of them all. I just adore Hialeah. When did you go there, today?"

"Yes, today. And all week."

"All week? Ooh, you must be a professional gambler."

"Not exactly."

"But going to the horse races all week—did you win?"

I thought, for the first time since the race, about money. I had lost $1,860 in five days. Joie de Vivre had won $1,800 of it back. What the hell. That was close enough.

"Not exactly," I said. "I broke even."

ABOUT THE AUTHOR

Joe McGinniss was born in New York City on December 9, 1942. He attended Holy Cross College and has worked on newspapers in Portchester, New York, Worcester, Massachusetts, and Philadelphia. His work has appeared in *Life, Harper's, New York Magazine, Sports Illustrated* and the *Saturday Evening Post*. Mr. McGinniss now lives in Blairstown, New Jersey.